Stacey and the Bad Girls

**Other books by
Ann M. Martin**

Stacey and the Bad Girls
Ann M. Martin

AN
APPLE
PAPERBACK

SCHOLASTIC INC.
New York Toronto London Auckland Sydney

Cover art by Hodges Soileau

ISBN 0-590-48237-8

12 11 10 9 8 7 6 5 4 3 2   5 6 7 8 9/9 0/0

Printed in the U.S.A.   40

First Scholastic printing, July 1995

The author gratefully acknowledges
Peter Lerangis
for his help in
preparing this manuscript.

Stacey and the Bad Girls

CHAPTER 1

"

. . . And the weather outlook for Stoney-brook is a high in the low eighties, with a slight chance of showers toward evening — "

Smack.

My palm landed on the snooze button of my clock radio. With a groan, I turned toward my bedroom wall.

My dream was fading. In it, I, Stacey McGill, was gliding over New York City at night with my boyfriend, Robert Brewster. (How were we doing this? Probably a magic carpet or something. I don't know. It was a dream.) We passed above West 81st Street, and I could see my old apartment building, glowing like an electronic toy.

As the clock radio went off, Robert and I were swooping down toward my former living room window.

But, of course, we never arrived.

Oh, well. It was time to wake up and pre-

1

pare for school anyway. I pulled my covers off, slid my feet to the floor, yawned, and staggered upright.

My eyes weren't totally functioning until I reached my door.

Unfortunately, neither was my brain. I suddenly remembered something extremely important.

It was summer vacation.

School was out.

I had set my alarm by mistake.

Duh.

I plopped back on my bed and tried to go to sleep again, but my dream was gone. And every time I drifted off, I could hear my mom rattling around in the kitchen, making herself breakfast.

By the time she left for work, I was wide awake.

As I rose out of bed, I spotted a letter from Robert on my desk. He had written it to me on one of the last days of school. *Hey, Toots!* it said across the top.

I smiled. "Toots" was what a grocer around the corner from my New York City apartment called all his female customers. (It drove everyone crazy.) I had imitated him for Robert, and he thought it was hilarious. Unfortunately, he started calling me Toots, too.

I hate that name.

2

But I forgive Robert. Besides, all I have to do is call him Dimples, and he stops.

I really wanted to see Robert that day, but he was helping some high school friends paint houses during the week — and of course, they were hired to paint this humongous mansion with about twenty-three miles of white wooden shingles.

So what else could I do that day? Not much. Call my friend Andi, who was leaving on a family vacation (lucky her). Do a little shopping, maybe. Find out if anyone wanted to hang with me this afternoon. Just another lazy Connecticut summer day.

New York City was still on my brain as I shuffled to my closet. When I lived in NYC, my summer days were *never* like this. They were jam-packed: tennis lessons in Central Park, weekend trips to Jones Beach, browsing in the Columbus Avenue shops, visiting Soho art galleries, lunching with Mom and my friends at the Garden Cafe in the Museum of Natural History.

Sigh.

Yes, I miss the Big Apple. (I bet you couldn't tell, right?) I can't help it. It's an awesome place. You simply cannot be bored there, even if you try. I should know. I lived there from birth until I was twelve (I'm thirteen now). Then came the Great Shuffle (my dad's company transferred him to Stoneybrook and then back to New York again) and the Big Chill (my parents divorced). All of a sudden, life was a mess. Mom and Dad had joint custody of me, and they gave me the choice of where to live — with Mom in Stoneybrook or with Dad in NYC. And I, Stacey McGill, the biggest New York lover in the world, chose Stoneybrook. Why? Mainly because of the friends I'd made here. Also, it's nice to walk outside and see thick, shady trees. (The trees in New York are scrawny. They have to be; otherwise their roots interfere with the underground wires and pipes.)

Do I ever regret my decision? You bet. Especially on a summer day with nothing to do.

I opened my closet door and looked at all my options. Jeans? Worn yesterday, with a U4Me T-shirt (U4Me is my current fave rock group). Flowered minidress? The day before. Black-striped baggy shorts? The day before that, with an oversize white sweatshirt.

I rummaged through a pile of T-shirts and some of last year's outfits. I tried on a pair of cream-colored drawstring pants, but they were so worn, the cream was beginning to yellow.

Finally I settled on a midnight-blue-and-white striped hooded sweatshirt with a laced placket, and matching Spandex leggings.

I looked in the mirror. I immediately wished

I hadn't. My hair looked like a blonde birds' nest, and I could go shopping with the bags under my eyes.

But my outfit was fine.

Do I sound too clothes-conscious to you? My mom thinks so. She has started calling my dressing ritual SDT, Stacey's Daily Trauma.

Well, I don't think it's a trauma at all. I enjoy it. I mean, choosing clothes is not like choosing vegetables or cans of soup. It's a skill. You have to take into account the season, the weather, your mood, and what you wore the previous day, just for starters. You know how it is.

Anyway, my outfit was sophisticated yet casual, with a nautical hint. Sort of like a summer day in NYC.

Sigh.

Okay. Now that I was put together, I could face the world. I headed downstairs, into the kitchen, and, after eating breakfast, made straight for the phone. First I tapped Andi Gentile's number.

"Hello?" Andi's voice replied.

"Hi, it's Stacey!" I said.

"Ohhhhhh . . . " she moaned. "I'm going to miss you!"

"Me, too," I said.

"You're going to miss you?"

"No! You know what I mean."

We both cracked up. Andi has a good sense of humor. She's one of my best post-Great Divide friends.

Oops. Let me back up. The Great Divide is not to be confused with the Great Shuffle and the Big Chill. The Great Divide happened when I left the Baby-sitters Club. Well, *left* and *was thrown out* at the same time. It was kind of mutual.

I loved being in the BSC. The members were my best friends. We went to school together (still do, when it's not summertime), had meetings three times a week, baby-sat together, even went on vacations together. You can't be much closer than that. As you can imagine, I devoted most of my free time to my friends. And I did, happily.

Then I met Robert, and everything started to change. I realized steady boyfriends and the BSC didn't necessarily mix. Not that I was the only BSC member with a steady guy. Mary Anne Spier has one, too, but her boyfriend is an associate member of the club (which I'll explain later). So Mary Anne can actually combine BSC time with boyfriend time. I couldn't, and I ended up trying to squeeze in both. It worked for awhile, but the more I got to know Robert and his friends, the more time I wanted to spend with them. I began arriving late for BSC meetings. I even missed a few. A couple of times, in order to go on dates, I arranged for another club member to take my sitting jobs.

My BSC friends started to resent me. Some of them would act weird whenever they saw me with my new friends. One of them, Dawn Schafer, actually spied on me from behind a jukebox when I was on a date. Can you believe the immaturity?

Anyway, the situation finally blew up over the dumbest thing. Robert and I threw a party, and I didn't invite all the BSC members. Why? First of all, I assumed they wouldn't want to come (they hadn't exactly been reaching out to Robert and our friends). Second, they'd been rude and babyish to me for weeks, and I was afraid they'd spoil the fun.

I ended up inviting only my best friend in the club, Claudia Kishi. Big mistake. The others found out and were hurt (and furious). Mary Anne and Dawn showed up at my door in the middle of the party, just to scold me.

The next BSC meeting was one of the low points of my life. Everyone screamed at me, and I just lost control. I can't even remember the horrible things I said. I quit and stormed out, while Kristy Thomas was telling me I was fired. (Kristy is the BSC president.)

Since then, the only BSC member who has even looked at me has been Claudia. We say hi and we've had a couple of good talks on the phone, but even that friendship has cooled off.

I sure have had a lot more free time since the Great Divide. I still baby-sit for one BSC sitting charge, Charlotte Johanssen (she's practically a sister), but I do miss regular baby-sitting. And, to be honest, I kind of miss my old friends, too.

My new friends, though, are fabulous. And of all the "Robert group," I like Andi the best. Saying good-bye to her was going to be so sad.

"What time do you have to leave?" I asked her.

"My mom's working a half day," she replied. "Dad says we have to be ready by about three o'clock."

"Want to come over for a good-bye lunch?" I asked. "I'm sure my mom wouldn't mind."

"Hang on." I heard a *clunk* as Andi put the receiver down. Then, after a muffled conversation with her dad, she said, "He says it's fine, as long as I'm back by two."

"I'll call everybody else," I said.

"Great! 'Bye! Thanks!"

I hung up, then quickly did a phone marathon: first Sheila MacGregor, then Heather Epstein, Mia Pappas, and Jacqui Grant.

I knew Sheila from homeroom. The others

were brand-new friends I'd met through Andi. Late in the school year, we'd all starting hanging out together. I still didn't know them as well as I knew Andi, so I was happy they were coming over.

That's the nice thing about an empty house in the summer. Everyone likes to visit you. (It helps to have a great mom who doesn't complain.)

Hmmm. Lunch for six. I checked around the kitchen. The refrigerator was pretty well stocked, but we needed some more bread, and we had very little good, old-fashioned junk food.

Actually, we never do have much junk food around, at least not the sweet stuff. That's because I have diabetes. My body can't control its own blood sugar, so I need to follow a strict diet and (are you sitting down?) inject myself daily with insulin. (I know, I know, it sounds disgusting, but believe me, you get used to it.)

I don't mind if people around me eat sweets, though. And I can eat chips and pretzels.

This was a clear cause for a shopping trip.

It was almost nine-thirty, and I'd invited everyone over for noon. I had just the right amount of time.

I ate a quick bowl of cereal, headed out to the garage, put on my HHH (Hideous Hairflattening Helmet), and hopped on my bike.

I adore riding through Stoneybrook on these cool, sleepy mornings. The streets are misty and green, and all you hear are a few crickets and an occasional lawn mower. It's almost enough to make me forget about NYC. Almost.

Downtown Stoneybrook was already pretty crowded with early shoppers. In Jugtown, a convenience store, I bought bagels, cream cheese, chips, and pretzels.

I took a slightly different route home, detouring past Bellair's, the department store where my mom works. I glided slowly past the display windows and checked out the bathing suits and summerwear. That, of course, was not the smartest idea, because all I wanted to do was run inside and buy clothes.

Somehow, bravely, I tore myself away. As I pedaled through the parking lot and onto the street, my mind was racing with new wardrobe ideas. I calculated how much a couple of bathing suits and a sundress would cost, then factored in my mom's employee discount and tacked on the tax. . . .

I wasn't really thinking about where I was going. If I had been, I might not have biked past the Rosebud Cafe. I might have remembered that Mary Anne's boyfriend, Logan Bruno, works there as a busboy. I might have steered away, as I'd been steering away from any contact with BSC members. (Not because I hate them or anything. I just like to avoid awkward meetings.)

Instead, with my mind full of numbers and beachwear, I sailed past the Rosebud. And I did see Logan inside, clearing a table.

Behind him, sipping sodas at the counter, were Mary Anne, Dawn, and Kristy.

Groan.

Did they see me? I don't know. I think Logan did, but I may be wrong.

My heart started pumping like crazy. I tore away from there.

Boy, did I feel weird. I mean, they had been my best friends. Not long ago I would have been happy to see them. Now I was running from them as if they had cooties.

When the Great Divide was happening, Mom used to say, "Don't worry. When one door closes, another one always opens." She's right. But sometimes I really miss my *old door* friends.

I smiled. My Old Door Friends. I wonder how they'd react to being called that.

CHAPTER 2

Kristy Thomas, for one, would hate the name. Not because it's insulting or stupid (which it is, I guess), but because she hadn't made it up.

Kristy is very competitive. Which is weird, because she sure doesn't need to be. She's absolutely brilliant. Not necessarily school brilliant, but idea brilliant. If she faces a problem, she solves it. If she faces no problem, she makes one, and *then* solves it.

Take the Baby-sitters Club, for instance. Kristy invented it. Why? Because one day she overheard her mom making a million calls trying to find a sitter for a time that neither Kristy nor her two older brothers could sit for David Michael, the youngest Thomas.

Kristy's solution: a centralized baby-sitter service, with one phone number.

That sounds like a great idea, if you're talking about a professional company. But Kristy wasn't. She meant kids her own age (twelve years old at the time), who went to school full-time and had family lives.

Well, she solved that problem, too. She dreamed up a whole structure for the BSC — meeting times, officers, rules, record-keeping, you name it.

Here's how it all works. The BSC meets three times a week, Mondays, Wednesdays, and Fridays, from five-thirty until six. Since Claudia's the only BSC member with a private phone line, meetings are held exclusively in her bedroom.

Okay, so it isn't perfect. It's not set up so parents can call round-the-clock. They have to memorize those three half hours. But you know what? No one seems to mind. The BSC has tons of clients. It's a great deal: make one phone call and reach seven excellent sitters.

And I mean seven. Kristy does not tolerate unnecessary absences. (Or latenesses. Believe me, I've tested her on both counts.)

What happens when a call comes in? Each job is assigned to a sitter and marked on a calendar. Then, after the job, the sitter has to write up her (or his) impressions and experiences in a notebook.

Pretty organized, huh? That's not all. Every member has a title, including five officers with special duties.

Kristy, as I mentioned before, is the BSC president. You would spot her easily at a meeting. She's the short, brown-haired one, sitting in a director's chair, wearing a visor and casual clothes (usually jeans and a T-shirt), and dominating everything. She can be very loud and bossy. Everyone likes her, though (I did, too, before she kicked me out of the BSC). And I have to admit she always dreams up great ideas for the club. She has organized talent shows, baby-sitting booths in local fairs, and all kinds of holiday events.

In her spare time, Kristy . . . competes. She's a sports fan, and she especially loves to play softball. She even coaches a softball team called Kristy's Krushers, which is made up of kids too young or too uncoordinated to join Little League.

Kristy's life is a rags-to-riches story. Soon after David Michael was born, Mr. Thomas abandoned the family. Kristy's mom raised four kids by herself and held down a good job. Then she married this millionaire named Watson Brewer, and the family moved into his mansion on the other side of town (Charlie, Kristy's oldest brother, drives her to meetings). Kristy's mother and Watson then adopted a little Vietnamese girl named Emily Michelle, and Kristy's grandmother moved in to help take care of her. Watson's two kids from a previous marriage live there every other month, so it's a pretty busy place.

The BSC vice-president is Claudia Kishi. Her main job is to let the club use her room and phone. But she's also a junk-food maniac, and very generous, so every meeting turns into pig heaven. Chunkies, Oreos, Ring-Dings, Twinkies, chips, pretzels — you can't turn around in that room without discovering something bad for your health. It's a wonder everyone hasn't turned into a blimp.

(Don't worry. I never ate any sweets. I was perfectly happy with the nonsugary snacks.)

Claudia has hair to die for, lustrous and jet-black. And despite the junk food, she looks like a model — thin figure, perfect skin. Honestly, I don't understand it. People's bodies are so strange. Mine can't handle sugar at all; Claud's must convert chocolate into wheat germ or something.

Claudia's junk food is carefully hidden, and so are her Nancy Drew mysteries. Huh? you may say. Well, you see, her parents are super-strict about "what goes into the mouth and what goes into the mind" (yes, her dad actually once said that). They permit only one kind of food (healthy) and three kinds of books (school books, great literature, and computer manuals).

Now, all of this is fine for Claud's older

sister, Janine, who takes college courses even though she's in high school. Her idea of a good time is extra-credit math problems. Mr. and Mrs. Kishi think she's perfect. They used to compare Claud to her constantly, which was totally unfair. Claudia's not the greatest student (you would not believe her spelling), but she's a talented and creative artist — in painting, sculpture, drawing, *and* jewelry-making. Kishi, by the way, is a Japanese name. Claud's grandparents were immigrants. Her mom's mom, Mimi, used to live with the Kishis. For a long time, Mimi was the only family member who really understood Claudia. When Mimi died, Claud was heartbroken.

Fortunately, Claud's parents have grown up a bit. They've started to realize how gifted their second daughter is.

But they still don't know about the junk food.

What was my job in the BSC? Glad you asked. I was treasurer, mainly because I really like math. Each Monday I collected dues (which, needless to say, was not a popular event). Why dues? To pay Claudia for the use of her phone. To give Kristy's brother Charlie gas money for driving Kristy to and from meetings. And to buy things for our Kid-Kits, which are boxes of games, toys, and books we sometimes take on jobs.

16

The BSC secretary is Mary Anne Spier. Her last name rhymes with *cheer*, not *crier*. Which, come to think of it, are both perfect words for Mary Anne. She's always cheerful, and she cries a lot. Sound like a contradiction? Not really. She's just intensely sensitive. Don't even try to watch a movie with her. I'm serious. During the sad parts you won't be able to hear a word over the sobbing. (Her boyfriend, Logan, takes a fistful of napkins with their popcorn, in case she runs out of tissues.)

Some other words to describe Mary Anne are quiet, thoughtful, and organized. She has completely mastered the world's most difficult, intimidating, complex book. The New York City white pages? The Bible? The collected theories of Albert Einstein? No, the Baby-sitters Club record book. Mary Anne has to keep track of the names and addresses of all our clients; the rates they pay; and their children's likes, dislikes, peculiarities, and birth dates. She also must know every BSC member's schedule — lessons, sports conflicts, doctor appointments, and so on. When a client calls, Mary Anne determines who's free to take the job, then offers it around, making sure to distribute work evenly. Then she records the job in the official BSC calendar, which is also in the book.

No, she does not go crazy. She likes being secretary.

Mary Anne is best friends with Kristy, which is proof that opposites attract. Well, not total opposites. They have a few things in common. They're both short (Mary Anne's a little taller). They have brown hair (Kristy's is longer). Each has a boyfriend (although Kristy and Bart Taylor are more like sports pals). And they both have had incredibly dramatic lives.

Soon after Mary Anne was born, her mom died. Mr. Spier was devastated. He wanted so badly to take care of his new baby, but he could barely think straight. Mrs. Spier's parents volunteered to raise Mary Anne until he felt more stable, and he agreed. But then, when he finally *was* ready, they refused to give Mary Anne back! They claimed he couldn't raise her alone adequately. Well, he said no way, José, and fought for her. But Mary Anne's grandparents must have scared him, because after he got her back, he went overboard trying to be Mr. Perfect Parent. To him, that meant rules, rules, and more rules. Up until she was in seventh grade, Mary Anne had a super-early bedtime and had to wear babyish dresses and keep her hair in pigtails. *Très* gross.

Eventually her father, Richard, did begin to let up a little. At the rate he was going, though, Mary Anne still might not have looked her age until college. But then something unexpected happened to Richard, and ever since, neither his nor Mary Anne's life has been the same.

What was the secret ingredient? LUV.

It started when Dawn Schafer moved here from California and joined the BSC. She and Mary Anne discovered a secret: Dawn's mom, who had grown up in Stoneybrook, had been high school sweethearts with Richard! But Dawn's grandparents were snobby and didn't think Richard was good enough for their daughter, so the romance was dashed on the rocks of forbidden love (I didn't make that up; I read it in a novel). After high school, the lovebirds lost touch. Dawn's mom went off to California and ended up marrying Mr. Schafer.

Fast-forward to the present. When Dawn and Mary Anne found out about this, they reintroduced their parents, and *shazam*, the sparks were visible in three states. (Well, I may be exaggerating a little. But they did fall in love again, and they were married.) Now Dawn and Mary Anne are stepsisters and their family lives in the Schafers' old farmhouse. (It is the coolest place. It's two hundred years old, with a tunnel that leads from a barn to Dawn's bedroom!)

Before I left the BSC, Dawn was the alternate officer. Her job was to take over whenever another officer was absent from a meeting. Now she has my job.

Dawn is the Eco-babysitter. She eats no red meat or sweets. She is passionate about organic gardening and animal rights and recycling and environmental awareness. And she'll bend your ear for an hour if you ask her about any of that stuff. (Do I sound a little touchy? Well, don't forget, Dawn was the one who spied on me in that restaurant.)

Anyway, Dawn has the most striking hair — practically down to her waist, and so blonde it's almost white. Her dad calls her Sunshine, and it's easy to see why. She has light skin, lots of freckles, and she smiles a lot.

The move to Stoneybrook wasn't easy for Dawn and her family. Her brother, Jeff (who's now ten years old), was miserable here. He began making trouble in school and constantly asking to move back in with his dad in California. Eventually Mrs. Schafer let him go. (Boy, was that a sad day.)

Dawn loved it here, but after awhile she also began missing California. So she ended up spending practically a whole semester there, and was the maid of honor at her dad's second wedding! According to Claudia, Dawn's been hinting that she wants to go back west again.

(If I were her mom, I think I'd be going crazy.)

Now that Dawn's the treasurer, who's the alternate officer? Shannon Kilbourne, who used to be an associate member, like Logan. Shannon goes to a private school called Stoneybrook Day. She's always busy with extracurricular activities there, but somehow she manages to find time for the BSC. (I don't know how she does it. She filled in for Dawn, too, when Dawn was in California.)

The BSC also has two junior members who happen to be best friends, Jessica Ramsey and Mallory Pike. Why "junior"? They're in sixth grade (everyone else is in eighth), and their parents don't let them baby-sit at night (except for their own siblings). They grumble about that a lot, but they do manage to do a lot of afternoon sitting, especially for Mallory's seven brothers and sisters.

You read that correctly. Seven (including a set of boy triplets). Mal's the oldest. Jessi also has younger siblings, but just two of them, a sister named Becca and a brother named Squirt. Jessi's African-American, and her family moved here from a place called Oakley, New Jersey. You should see her dance. She takes advanced ballet lessons, and she's soooo talented. Mal is Caucasian, with curly reddish brown hair and glasses, and she grew up in Stoneybrook. She's shy and even-tempered, and she loves to write and illustrate her own stories.

With Kristy's ideas, Claudia's art, Jessi's dancing, and Mal's storymaking, BSC should probably stand for Being So Creative.

As I biked away from the Rosebud Cafe, other appropriate abbreviations popped into my head. A good club motto: Bring Some Children. A description of our meetings: Butter, Salt, and Candy. A benefit of being a babysitter: Building Self-Confidence.

I had an urge to turn around and share some of these with my ex-friends at the Rosebud. But I didn't. I mean, they were my ex-friends for a good reason.

As I thought of that, another abbreviation occurred to me.

Better Stay Clear.

CHAPTER 3

" 'I don't wanna say good-byyyyyye . . . ' " Heather Epstein sang, twanging her air guitar.

" 'Good-byyye . . . ' " Mia Pappas echoed.

" 'So I'll turn back and sayyyyyy . . . ' " Jacqui Grant chimed in.

" 'And sayyyyy . . . ' " I joined Mia in the chorus.

" 'Never — ' " we all started to sing. But no one continued. Instead we burst into giggles.

We were singing a U4Me song as a farewell to Andi. Only none of us had stopped to consider the line that followed: "Never come back into my life!"

Some farewell song.

Sheila MacGregor was sprawled on the kitchen floor, cracking up. Andi was still sitting at the table, laughing so hard she was coughing. "Thanks a lot!" she said.

"Sorry," I said. Then I sang, "Pleeeeeease come back — "

"Into my liiiiiife!" everyone else joined in. We gave ourselves a big hand.

Andi was moist-eyed. "You guys," she said with a huge, embarrassed grin.

"Uh-oh!" Sheila exclaimed. "Is she going to cry?"

"It's just the onions," Andi insisted, pointing to a small stack I'd sliced.

"Where's your camera, Stace?" Jacqui teased.

"*Augggh*, don't!" Andi protested, wiping her eyes with a napkin.

I laughed. "It's on my bedroom closet shelf."

I rose to get it, but Jacqui was up the stairs like a shot.

"Woofayfa goosha," mumbled Heather with a mouthful of chips.

Mia rolled her eyes. "Where'd you learn manners?"

Heather swallowed. "I said, we'll take a group shot. Don't worry, Andi. We won't embarrass you."

"Oh, yes, we will," Sheila added.

You know what I appreciate most in a friendship? Not nice clothes or a taste for U4Me, but a sense of humor. That's one of the things I like best about Claudia. And one of the reasons I was psyched about my new

24

friends. They were turning out to be pretty funny, too.

Funny, but not at all like my BSC friends. What *are* they like? Well, Andi's sort of normal-looking, with dark brown hair and a wide smile. Jacqui has this constant sly grin, dark red hair streaked with green, and pale white skin. Also, she wears nose jewelry. Mia is tall and skinny and likes black clothes and black lipstick. Heather has short, spiky brown hair and loves the grunge look. Sheila's blonde and very athletic. She's on the cheerleading squad.

Cheerleading, by the way, almost destroyed my friendship with Sheila before it started. I tried out for the squad during basketball season and was rejected (mainly because one of the girls had a crush on Robert). Boy, was that experience eye-opening. I realized that almost the entire school was treating the players and cheerleaders like gods. They took advantage of it, too — skipping classes and copying other kids' homework, while everyone turned the other way. It was *so* unfair. Anyway, Robert felt the way I did; he even quit the basketball team in protest. Needless to say, it was awhile before Sheila and I patched things up, but we managed.

I sat down again and slathered some cream cheese onto half a sesame bagel. Sheila and

Heather were digging into the chips again as Andi and Mia gabbed away.

Upstairs I heard Jacqui laughing out loud in my room. A moment later she bounded down, holding my camera and grinning wickedly.

"What's so funny?" I asked.

"Nothing," she replied.

For *nothing* she sure was turning red.

The next thing I knew, she held the camera out to me and said, "Here you go, Toots."

Oh, my lord. Robert's letter! It was still on my desk.

"You didn't . . ." I said.

"Stacey, I cannot believe Robert calls you Toots!" Jacqui could barely get the words out before convulsing with laughter.

Sheila practically spit out her Arizona Iced Tea. Mia and Heather looked dumbfounded.

"It was a joke," I said.

But could I explain the whole story? No way. My friends were howling.

"Sweet Toots McGill!" Sheila crowed.

I shot Jacqui a look.

"Sorry," she said with a guilty smile. "I know, I was a snoop. But I couldn't help it. It was just lying there."

With a sigh, I took the camera from her. I began doing the only thing I could do — taking pictures of the entire pack of hyenas.

You know what? Not everyone looks gorgeous while shrieking with laughter, eyes closed, mouths full of food. In fact, some of the shots were downright humiliating. Which was just fine.

Call it Toots's Revenge.

After all the hysterics, we had a tearful good-bye with Andi. Right away I missed her terribly, but I was psyched about growing closer to the other girls, despite Jacqui's sneakiness (I mean, it was partially my fault for leaving the letter out). During the rest of the day I read and sunbathed and yawned a lot. Ho-hum.

The next day, when Sheila called to suggest that everyone come over again, the word "Sure!" just rocketed out of my mouth.

"It's soooo great you have that empty house all summer," she remarked.

"Uh-huh," I replied. "If you like silence and loneliness."

Sheila laughed. "Hey, we can take care of that. I'll bring over my tape. It's totally, one hundred percent U4Me. I keep it in the VCR and press record each time one of their videos comes on. I have every single one, including a garage video they made when they were just starting out. And Skyllo? His real name is Aristotle Dukas! Disgusting or what? Anyway, I also recorded MTV's exclusive interview with him!"

"Cool," I said. "Come over any time."

"Okay. I'll call the others. See you."

A video full of U4Me? I could deal with an afternoon of that.

Skyllo, by the way, is the name of U4Me's lead singer. You would not believe his eyes. They're huge and vulnerable and strong and when you see them on TV they pull you right out of your seat. (Okay, I'm exaggerating, but just barely.) On a hunkiness scale of 1 (bowser) to 10 (turbo-hunk) he rates about a 15. His fan club has a waiting list. If I ever meet him in person, it'll be heart attack time. Plop goes Stacey onto the floor.

Do I sound like a groupie? Well, sorry, but I simply cannot have enough of U4Me. They are the coolest group. My mom thinks I'm ridiculous. But you should see pictures of her from the sixties and seventies. She was a Beatles fanatic. She even called herself Paula for awhile, to honor Paul McCartney. Can you imagine? Anyway, she just cannot sit still for something a little more up-to-date. She calls me a "grunge sponge," and U4Me isn't really a grunge band! They just sing the best songs.

Sheila is the biggest fan of all of us. She has actually written to Skyllo five times (and received five identical autographed black-and-white photos).

Around two-thirty, Heather arrived at my house, followed by Jacqui, Mia, and Sheila.

The tape was the first order of business.

We crowded onto the sofa. When U4Me appeared on the TV, Mia let out a squeal of excitement.

We watched the entire thing — two hours, including many repeats of music videos. We were in couch potato heaven.

During something that Sheila had recorded just that morning, a veejay began announcing the upcoming U4Me tour schedule. We all sat up and leaned forward. Sheila turned up the volume to max.

"Currently playing to sold-out houses in Seattle, U4Me will swing south to L.A. for three huge performances, after which they'll hit Denver, St. Louis, Minneapolis, Chicago, and Milwaukee. The rest of the stops are under negotiation. . . ."

"They're getting closer," Jacqui said.

"Say Stamford!" Heather yelled at the TV.

"Don't hold your breath," said Mia. "They're only doing big cities."

"So what are we," I asked, "chopped liver?"

Mia laughed. Sheila stared at me as if I'd just said something in Sanskrit. The others kept watching the tube.

(Well, I can't help it. My dad uses that expression all the time. I think it's hysterical.)

About the fifth time the "I Don't Wanna Say Good-bye" video came on, Mia disappeared into the kitchen. She returned with a bowlful of peanuts.

"Yum!" Jacqui exclaimed.

"These were in your pantry, Stace, way in the back behind all the soup cans," Mia said. "It's okay, right?"

I nodded. I guessed it was okay. I hadn't expected her to go into the pantry, but hey, the nuts were for eating, weren't they?

We watched and munched. We sang along. We discussed the newly shaved head of Ran Philips, another U4Me singer, and decided it looked more like a kiwi fruit than a football. Then we rewound and watched our favorite parts again.

When the peanuts were gone, Heather took a quart container of yogurt from the fridge and Mia found a bag of blue corn chips.

Yogurt, chips, peanuts. I ran down the list of food to replace.

An hour or so later, when everyone was leaving, I left with them. As we walked to the garage for our bikes, Mia asked, "Where are you going?"

"To the store," I replied. I didn't exactly want to say, *To replace the stuff you guys ate.*

That would be *très* tacky, as if I were trying to make them feel guilty (although it would have been nice if they'd offered to buy the stuff themselves).

"I'll go with you," Jacqui volunteered.

"Me, too," Heather said.

"Well, uh — " I began.

"Race!" Sheila called out.

"Oh, please," Mia said. "It's too hot. Let's just ride like normal people."

I was stuck. They were going to join me.

So what did I do? Detour.

As we chatted, I led everyone on a long, winding tour through the shady streets . . . and guess what? We just happened to ride past the house Robert was painting. (What a coincidence, huh? Nudge, nudge.) We hung out for awhile, until Robert's boss started grunting impatiently. Then we headed to the strip mall for a snack.

Before I knew it, it was time to go home and greet Mom.

I never did buy the chips, yogurt, and peanuts. But no big deal. That could wait. I had had a great couple of days. And I was discovering something important.

The summer might not have to be a bore after all.

* * *

Wednesday made it three days in a row. Three consecutive visits from my new friends, three rescues from summer slump. Heather, Mia, Jacqui, and I tore through a few fashion magazines, then started making a scrapbook of U4Me clippings.

At around four o'clock, the bell rang.

I ran to the door, pulled it open — and came face to face with the speckled beast of Stoneybrook.

"Boo," said Robert. His face and hair were covered with dried spatters of white paint. His T-shirt and shorts were smeared. I don't even want to describe the grossness of his sneakers.

"Ewwww!" cried Sheila. "Robert Brewster, couldn't you change first?"

"Sorry," Robert replied. "My boss had to leave early, so he gave me a ride. I figured I'd stop over and say hi. But, hey, if you want me to go . . ."

He started to turn, but I pulled him back. "No, it's okay! Don't listen to them."

As Robert walked in, I grabbed the newspaper from an end table and spread it over the sofa.

"Uh, it's dry, Stace," Robert said.

"Just in case," I replied.

"Stacey, you are sooo middle class," Mia said with a snort.

Robert was already wolfing down pretzels.

"Yeah? What are you, Mia? *Upper* or something?"

"Oh, please," Mia groaned.

"Would you pass the caviar, please?" Robert asked in a terrible British accent.

Mia picked up a plum and threw it at him.

Robert ducked. The plum bounced off the top of the couch and splatted against the wall.

"Oops, I'll clean it up!" Giggling, Mia stood up and ran into the kitchen.

"Call your butler!" Robert teased.

"Robert, chill," Sheila said, pronouncing his name the French way, Ro-*bear*.

"Sorry." Robert shrugged. "So, what have you guys been doing?"

"Looking at clothes and making a U4Me scrapbook," Jacqui replied.

Robert hopped to his feet. "Well, see you!"

(Robert does not like U4Me. But nobody's perfect.) I convinced him to stay awhile, which was fun, except for the fact that he ate every remaining bit of food on the table. (Robert has a huge appetite. He makes Claudia seem picky.)

He left around five. At five-thirty, Mom came home. "Hel*looo*!" she sang, walking through the front door.

I was lying on the floor. Heather was sitting crosswise in an armchair. Mia was lying on the sofa, and Jacqui was walking in from the kitchen, chewing on something.

Everyone sat up. Mom stopped in her tracks. She looked around, smiling.

Now, I know my mom. She has many different kinds of smiles. This one was of the "What on earth has been going on here?" variety.

"Hi, Mom," I said cheerily.

"So, you're having a party?" she asked.

I shrugged. "Just hanging out."

The coffee table was covered with crumbs and half-empty plates. A couple of plastic cups were on the mantel, a couple more on chair arms. The plum had left a dark circle on the wall. And I hadn't yet removed Robert's newspaper from the sofa.

Mom lifted the paper and peered at it in dismay. "Is this today's?" she asked.

"Oops," I said.

"Uh, I have to go," Heather blurted out, scrambling for the door. "Nice to see you, Mrs. McGill."

"And what is this?" Mom was now scrutinizing a large white blotch on the wooden floor, just outside the area rug.

The paint was dry, huh? I made a mental note to scold Robert about that.

"Gee, already five-thirty?" Jacqui piped up. "Dinnertime! See you!"

"Wow, me, too," Mia added with a nervous giggle. "Peace, guys."

Whoosh. Exit friends.

It was just me, Mom, and the mess. "I'm sorry, Mom, we — "

Mom held up an empty can of macadamia nuts and a half-finished bag of vegetable chips. "I guess this is where all the food has been going," she said.

"Well, yeah — "

"Like the low-fat yogurt I couldn't find this morning?"

I nodded. "We ate that, too, but I'll replace it all. I promise!"

"Is this what you do all day, hang around the house and feed your friends? Don't you have anything better to do with your time?"

I thought for a moment. It was a good question. "No," I answered plainly.

"Well, *I* do." Mom scooped up some trash and huffed off to the kitchen. "I think it's time you got a job, young lady!"

CHAPTER 4

" 'Nutrition consultant,' " I read from a help wanted ad in the *Stoneybrook News*. "I could do that!"

Mom peered over my shoulder. "Keep reading."

" 'Flx hrs, sal neg, min 5 yrs exp.' " (I tried to pronounce this as best as I could.) "What's a flx hr?"

"Flexible hours, salary negotiable, minimum five years' experience," Mom patiently translated.

"Oops."

To tell you the truth, I was excited about the idea of a job. Hanging out at home was fun, but I could see that it might become boring, every single day, even with good friends. (Besides, it could send our food budget through the roof.)

"The problem is," Mom muttered, "most of

these are full-time positions, for adult workers."

"Here's one!" I exclaimed. " 'PT.' That's part-time, right? 'Nursery and Floral Deliv; friendly, good ap; Class 3 lic req.' It's perfect! What's a Class Three lic?"

"I believe that's a truck driver's license."

"Oh."

Mom ran her index finger down the page. "There must be something appropriate, like a mother's helper . . ."

"Forget it. The BSC locks all those jobs up."

Mom looked at me. "Well, you could talk to Kristy again."

"Mo-*om*!"

"Just suggesting." She went back to the ads. "Ah-ha! A paper route!"

My stomach sank. "Oh, puh-leeze! Have you ever seen a kid at the end of a paper route? I mean, smudge city! I might as well work in a coal mine!"

Mom gave an exasperated sigh. "You don't want to paint houses. You don't want to deliver papers. You won't patch things up with the Baby-sitters Club. You know, there isn't much else a thirteen-year-old can do, Stacey."

As we continued looking through the ads, my mind was working. As usual, in times of crisis, I asked myself the most important question: *What would Kristy do?*

For one thing, she'd probably make an advertisement for herself. EAGER, ENERGETIC, FRIENDLY, BRIGHT, GENERALLY WONDERFUL THIRTEEN-YEAR-OLD WILLING AND ABLE TO DO ANYTHING, something like that. Then she'd post the ad in all the places we used to advertise the Baby-sitters Club: at school, in pediatricians' offices, in the mall, on supermarket bulletin boards . . .

That gave me an idea.

"Let's go to the supermarket!" I said to my mom.

"Don't worry about the food," she replied. "First things first."

"I mean, to look at the ads, Mom! Maybe I'll find something there."

A smile crept across Mom's face. "Heyyy, now you're cooking."

We went right out to the car and drove to the store. The bulletin board was jammed with index cards. It was a complete jumble. Pianos, pets, cars, furniture, plants, and computers for sale. Software experts, mechanics, dog groomers, and interior designers available for hourly rates. I even discovered an old BSC flier, shot through with thumbtack holes.

Mom and I found four possibilities:

1) A woman named Myrtle wanted a part-time companion for her elderly mother.

2) A "start-up" modeling agency invited

"clean-cut types, ages ten to fifteen" to apply, "no experience necessary."

3) A "two-income couple" needed a dog walker twice a day.

4) A place called SportsTown in Mercer advertised for part-time help at their "Toddler Center."

I wrote down all four phone numbers. I was dying to make the calls that night, but Mom said it was too late.

I could hardly sleep. I awoke at seven, but Mom warned me not to call anyone until after nine, to be courteous.

Sheila called at eight-fifty-five, just after Mom left for work. "Stacey, I did it!" she squealed.

"Did what?" I asked.

"Convinced my mom to let me have my nose pierced!"

"Oh." Lovely. (Okay, okay, I'm old-fashioned. I mean, nose jewelry looks cool on some people, like Jacqui, but it is definitely NMS, Not My Style.)

"Want to come with me to the piercing place?" she asked.

"I'd love to, but my mom wants me to find a job. I have to make calls today."

"Gross. Well, call me later."

"Cool. Wish me luck."

"Good luck!"

As soon as I hung up, I took a deep breath and called Myrtle's number.

"Hello?" a clipped voice answered.

"Hi, my name is Stacey McGill, and I'm calling in response to the ad you placed in the supermarket, about the position for — "

"Yes, I'm aware of the position. What are your qualifications, Tracey?"

"Uh, *Stacey*. I'm very neat, and I adore older people, and I — "

"Experience?" she interrupted.

"Excuse me?"

"What's your experience in elder care, dear?"

"Well, uh, none. I've done a lot of baby-sitting — "

"Thank you, young lady, but I am decidedly not looking for a baby-sitter."

"Okay. Well, thanks. 'Bye."

Click.

Oh for one.

I tried the dog couple next, and an answering machine picked up:

"You have reached the Frampson residence," a chirpy voice said. "Neither Hubert, Melissa, nor Cutesy can come to the phone now. Please leave a message after the bark." Then, after some muffled mumbling: *"ROWWWWWWF!"*

Cutesy sounded humongous. I had second

thoughts. But I left my name and number anyway.

Next I tried SportsTown. The guy who answered seemed interested in my baby-sitting experience. He said I could visit anytime until eight o'clock at night "and ask for Otto."

A lead! I told him I'd ask Mom to drive me there that night.

Suddenly I felt much more confident. And I needed to, because I was on the verge of skipping the next call.

Bravely, I tapped out the number of the modeling agency.

"Hello, Sylphide Models," a British-accented woman's voice said.

"Hi." I was so nervous, I sounded like a Munchkin. "My name is Stacey McGill, and I'm responding to your ad?"

"Yes, Stacey, do you have a portfolio?"

"Well, no, but the ad said — "

"No experience necessary." The woman chuckled warmly. "That's right. Well, we're at Thompson and Main, and I can see you at eleven-fifteen today if you can make it, or — "

"Fine!" I blurted out. The address was close to downtown Stoneybrook. An easy bike ride.

When I hung up, I was shaking. Eleven-fifteen? It was already ten. I really had to move.

I stormed upstairs, showered, blow-dried my hair, and put on a little makeup.

Then I ransacked my closet.

Clean-cut. I had to look clean-cut. What did that mean? Shorts? Slacks? Cheerleader outfit? *You should have asked*, I scolded myself.

Well, duh. I wasn't exactly going to call back.

This was a major SDT. In minutes my bed was piled high with clothes. I finally settled on a simple floral-patterned sundress — young, carefree, pretty.

As I ran out of the house, my heart was pounding. *Slow down*, I told myself. *They said clean-cut, not sweat-soaked.*

I hopped on my bike, and started pedaling slowly.

I arrived at Sylphide way too early. Three other girls were waiting, accompanied by their mothers. Each girl was carrying a huge leather portfolio, wearing a gorgeous outfit, and looking like a Sassy cover.

I felt like a toad. I kept my mouth shut for fear that a "Ribit" would emerge.

The time dragged. I could feel myself slowly melting. Aging. Like cheese. I thought the interview would never happen.

Then, when I was finally called, I faced a young man and woman, sitting across a table from me. They were dressed in black. We spoke a little, and then the man lifted a Polaroid camera and asked me to smile.

I tossed back my hair and tried to think of something funny.

" 'Atta girl," he said. The flash nearly blinded me.

"Thank you," the woman chimed in. "We'll be in touch if we need you."

"Is that it?" I asked. "I mean, do I make it?"

The woman's smile stiffened. "Well, dear," she said, watching my Polaroid develop, "I'm not sure I'd go fashion or high-end with you, but we are thinking of expanding into product modeling."

"I see her as girl-next-door, household product, lawn care, possibly snack food," the guy said.

"Mm-hm," the woman said absently. "Thank you, dear."

That *Thank you* sounded an awful lot like *Good-bye*.

"You're wel– I mean, thank you," I stammered, scooting out as fast as I could.

"I wouldn't put your eggs in that basket," Mom said gently when I described the modeling interview over dinner. "I think SportsTown is a better shot."

I wolfed down my meal.

As soon as we finished, Mom drove me

there. What a cool place — a warehouse full of pinball machines, video games, batting cages, and miniature golf. In one corner was an enormous play area that resembled a compressed, three-floor house made of rubber padding and soft plastic mesh, with steps and corkscrew slides and small pits full of multicolored plastic balls. A few kids my age were stationed inside the contraption at different levels, probably to help out kids who felt lost or scared.

This job would be perfect.

Otto was a sweet man with a mustache, receding hairline, and pot belly. He took Mom and me into a small office and gave me a form to fill out.

When I finished, he looked over my application and smiled. "Very nice, Stacey. I'll put it on file and we'll see what comes up."

Then he opened a file drawer and stuck the sheet in the back of an enormous folder.

"All of those are applications?" I asked.

Otto gave me a sympathetic smile. "I'm afraid so. But a lot of the applicants find other work, or change their minds, or have conflicts. So we could be calling you as early as . . . I don't know, September, maybe."

Oh, terrific.

I forced my lips into a smile shape and

thanked him. Then Mom and I trudged back to the car.

"September?" I mumbled as Mom drove off. "I'll be in college before he calls."

Mom sighed. "Oh, well, there's always Cutesy."

Cutesy did not call back. But her owner, Melissa, did. At eight-thirty on Friday morning, just after Mom left for work.

Melissa seemed very friendly and eager, until she asked what my age was, and I told her thirteen.

"Oh, dear," she replied. "Well, I had in mind someone — um, you don't happen to have an older sister or cousin, do you? I mean, I do have to be able to trust someone with a set of keys."

I said I was sorry. And I was. She was my last hope.

Back to the drawing board.

Rrrriiiing!

I jumped.

It's Sylphide! was my first thought.

Chill, Stacey, was my second. I waited until the second ring, picked up the receiver smoothly, and said "Hello?" in my most nonchalant voice.

"Stacey? Are you okay? You sound scared."

Thank you, Mia. "Hi. I'm fine. What's up?"

"Mom's driving Jacqui and Heather and me to the mall. Want to come? We're meeting Sheila there."

"Oooh, yeah! How's her nose?"

"Didn't happen. Her mom thought she wanted another hole in her *ear*. Sheila went ballistic, but she's okay now. We'll pick you up in a half-hour, okay?"

"Great."

The car arrived an hour later. Mia's mom, who was dressed in a madras sundress and espadrilles, carried on a conversation about U4Me with us throughout the drive. At the mall, she helped Mia buy a black leather vest and purple spray for her hair.

Go figure.

When I was dropped at home after our trip, I ran straight to our phone machine. Zero messages.

Ugh.

I flopped down on the living room sofa with a handful of magazines. I was halfway through the latest *Life* when the front door burst open.

"Hi, darling!" Mom said brightly. "Guess what?"

"What?" I mumbled.

Mom knelt next to me, grinning. "Well, that Toddler Center at SportsTown gave me an idea. I went to the new Kid Center at Bellair's — you know, on the third floor? And guess who needs a young part-time aide to help out during the busy hours?"

I sat up. "No!"

"Yes! I set you up for an interview with Ms. Blair, the personnel director, first thing in the morning."

Well, talk about insomnia. I tried counting sheep but gave up when I reached 1,137.

Strangely, I felt great on Saturday morning. Mom drove me to Bellair's and brought me to the office of Ms. Blair, who was young, with a friendly smile and curly hair that fell to her eyes.

"So, Stacey, your mom tells me you're great with kids," Ms. Blair said, looking at a page of handwritten notes. "You belong to a baby-sitters club?"

"Well, I did — "

"Wonderful!" She pushed a small folder my way. "Why don't you fill out these forms, and I'll bring Mrs. Grossman in here. She's in charge of the Kid Center."

As I carefully followed her instructions, a tall, gray-haired woman in crisp jeans and a gingham shirt bounded into the room. "Well, bless her, she does look like her mother."

Mrs. Grossman introduced herself to me, waited until I finished with the forms, and walked me to the top floor.

I hadn't seen the Kid Center before. It was much larger than the Toddler Center at SportsTown, and the play areas were spread around — a mesh-enclosed pit of plastic balls, padded tunnels, a train-and-truck corner, dollhouses, arts-and-crafts tables, and a few trikes and wagons.

"It's fantastic," I remarked.

"The materials are state of the art," Mrs. Grossman explained. "Lightweight, durable, safe. The lighting is optimal for young eyes, and our regular staff all have primary-education —"

A little girl, the only "customer" in the place, toddled up to me, dragging a Raggedy Ann doll. "Dolly play?" she said.

I smiled. "Excuse me," I said to Mrs. Grossman. I followed the girl to the dollhouse, where she had set up some plastic figures, GI Joes, and Matchbox cars. "Oh, are you having a party?" I guessed.

"Birfday," she replied.

We held an elaborate little celebration that involved using a rubber mailbox as a birthday cake. I guess I kind of lost track of why I was there. Halfway through the party, Mrs. Grossman knelt down beside me. I'd completely forgotten she was in the room. I'd been ignoring her.

"Uh, Stacey?" she whispered.

"Oh! Sorry, Mrs. Grossman!" I exclaimed, whirling around.

"It's okay. You can stay if you want," she replied. "How does Monday morning sound, around ten? Your regular time will be eleven, but on the first day you can ease into the routine when it's quieter."

"You mean, I — I have the . . ."

She put her hand on my shoulder and smiled. "Welcome to Bellair's, Stacey."

CHAPTER 5

Saturday

Can I write about Amy?
I mean, I _am_ sitting for
her, right?

This book is for BSC jobs, Dawn. You
know that. Amy is your cousin.

Oh, Kristy. For a smart
person, you can be such
a poop.

It takes one to

Official note: I, Dawn
Schafer, aware of possible
harsh penalty, am writing
this behind Kristy Thomas's
back. But I can't help it.
The last time I saw Amy,
she was in diapers. Now

she's six and almost four feet tall and learning to read. I'm sooooo excited.

Now, if only she felt that way. . . .

I was ecstatic about my job. I called Claudia to tell her about it. Later on, she read Dawn's BSC notebook entry to me. Then she told me about the whole adventure.

Amy's dad and Dawn's mom are cousins. That makes Amy a *second* cousin of Dawn. The Porters live in Chicago, and Dawn's family had been out of touch with them for years, because Mr. Porter didn't get along with Dawn's dad. (Mr. Porter's an executive for a meat-packing company, which may be another reason Dawn has never talked about that branch of the family.)

Anyway, Sharon (Dawn's mom) had sent the Porters a wedding announcement. Since then, Mr. Porter had been calling regularly. Lately the cousins had been discussing a visit.

One night, while Dawn was helping clean up after dinner, she overheard one of those calls: "Hello, Ed!" Sharon said. "Yes . . . terrific. . . . When are we going to see you? . . . Oh? How long? . . . Here? Uh-huh. . . . No, I'm sure Dawn would be delighted. . . . Well, I'll have to talk to Richard, okay? I'll get back to you. 'Bye."

Dawn, Mary Anne, and Richard were staring at her as she hung up.

Sharon looked stunned. "Ed's been offered a three-week business trip to Europe, starting in a week. He says he hasn't traveled with Rochelle since their honeymoon, so he wants to take her and leave Amy with us."

"What?" Richard exclaimed.

"Yeeeeaaaa!" Dawn shouted.

"He doesn't think Amy would enjoy the trip," Dawn's mom went on. "He says he'd completely understand if we couldn't handle it, but he's dying for the families to become closer. He and Rochelle would fly to New York and take a train to Stoneybrook, then leave Amy here and return to New York for their flight."

"Well, one week is awfully short notice," Richard humphhed. "And with both of us working full-time — "

"No problem," Dawn cut in. "Mary Anne and I can take care of her. She could stay in Jeff's room."

"Yeah, it would be fun!" Mary Anne said.

"But we hardly even know these people,"

Richard continued. "And three weeks of child care is a lot to ask."

"*These people* are my cousins, dear," Sharon patiently reminded him. "And they're awfully nice."

"Please, Dad," Mary Anne pleaded. "Can we?"

"Pleeeeeeeease?" Dawn echoed.

Richard looked at the girls and sighed. "Let me take it under advisement." (That's lawyer talk for "I'll discuss it with your mother in private.")

You know who won the argument.

Well, Dawn and Mary Anne were thrilled. They immediately went to work preparing the house.

First order of business, Jeff's room. It was all wrong for a six-year-old girl. Down went the Kung Fu posters, Los Angeles Dodgers team picture, and Boston Red Sox dartboard. Off came the Darth Vader bedsheets. The Marvel superhero stickers were tough to scrape off, so Dawn covered them with animal stickers from the National Wildlife Federation. Mary Anne moved a lot of books and magazines to the attic, keeping some good ones such as *Freckle Juice*, *Esio Trot*, and *The Lorax* for Amy.

(When Jeff found out about all this, he was furious.)

Step Two. Sharon drove Dawn and Mary Anne to the mall, where they bought some colorful cat-pattern sheets, a few books (including easy readers), art supplies, and toys.

On the way home, they could not stop talking.

"Okay, Saturday'll be yakking and eating and getting acquainted," Dawn said. "Sunday afternoon we can take her to the movies, and maybe lunch at Cabbages and Kings."

"How about the art museum?" Mary Anne suggested.

"Great! Then that night we'll play Pictionary Junior."

"Monday we can take her to the Stones' farm."

"And Carle Playground."

"Maybe Laurel and Patsy Kuhn can eat over that night."

"Whoa!" Sharon cut in. "Spread things out. You're already running the poor girl ragged."

As they pulled up the driveway, Richard was grinning proudly on the front lawn, holding a small girls' bike with multicolored tassels attached to the handles.

"Where'd you get that?" Mary Anne called out.

"One of the junior partners at work," Richard replied. "His daughter grew out of it."

"All *riiiiight!*" Dawn whooped.

"Dad, that's so sweet!" Mary Anne said.

Richard smiled. "Well, she's my family, too, you know."

Throughout the week, Dawn and Mary Anne put up posters in Amy's room. They lined Amy's shelves with toys and books donated by baby-sitting charges who'd grown out of them. Then Dawn and Mary Anne wrapped a huge red ribbon around the bike, and bought a sachet to put in Amy's closet.

Thursday afternoon, when they returned from a shopping trip, the answering machine had a message for Dawn:

"Hi, it's Sunny Winslow," said a faint, gloomy voice. "Dawn . . . um, please call right away. It's . . . just call, okay?" *Click*.

Mary Anne looked worried. "She sounds awful."

Dawn dropped her bags on the counter and ran right to the phone. Sunny is her best friend in California, and she's usually cheerful and outgoing.

Dawn tapped out the number. "Hello?" Sunny said.

"Hi, it's me, Dawn!"

"Ohhhhhh." Sunny's voice trailed off into a quiet sob.

"Sunny, are you okay?" Dawn asked.

"I — I am," Sunny stammered. "But my mom's sick."

"What happened?"

"Well, remember when she used to smoke? You know, she started when she was our age. And now, her lungs . . ."

Dawn felt her stomach clench. "Cancer?" she whispered.

Immediately she wished she hadn't said that. Sunny burst into tears. "The doctors don't know how far it's spread," she whispered. "Maybe it's not too bad. We don't know. It's all so confusing. I'm sorry. I just had to call someone."

"It's okay," Dawn reassured her. "I'm glad it was me."

For an hour or so, Dawn patiently listened and tried to give Sunny support. But after they hung up, Dawn starting crying, too.

Slowly, she told her mom and Mary Anne what had happened.

Tears streaming down her cheeks, Mary Anne put an arm around Dawn. "I'm so sorry."

"I just have to go back there," Dawn said. "I have to be there for her."

Sharon's eyes dropped downward. She gave her daughter a long squeeze, then stood up and started putting the groceries away.

* * *

Dawn decided not to bring up a trip to California again, at least not until after Amy's visit. She knew how sensitive Sharon was about "losing" Jeff to the West Coast and giving up Dawn for extended visits.

But still, all through the next day Dawn could hardly think of anything else.

On Saturday morning, Dawn threw herself into final preparations for Amy's arrival. She and Mary Anne put a small bouquet of flowers in Amy's room and made a *Welcome, Cousin Amy!* banner to string across the living room.

While Sharon drove to the train station to pick up the Porters, Dawn and Mary Anne showered and dressed up. Richard, who has become an excellent cook, made a salad Niçoise (and a peanut-butter-and-jelly sandwich, just in case).

Dawn was setting out chips and nuts on the living room coffee table when the doorbell rang.

She, Mary Anne, and Richard ran for the door. Dawn arrived first and pulled it open.

"Hiiiiii!"

The Porters and the Spiers had a huge hugfest. Ed was a loud, bearlike guy; Rochelle was elegant and sweet. Amy, with freckles and reddish-brown hair tied with a bow, wore a summery Laura Ashley dress. She clung to her mom's skirt as they walked inside.

"Amy, you are such a big girl now!" Dawn exclaimed.

"She's reading, too!" Ed said.

Amy nodded shyly.

As Richard took Amy's luggage into the house, Sharon and the grown-ups sat on the living room sofa and chairs. They looked at wedding photos, oohed and ahhhed over Dawn and Amy, tried to get to know Mary Anne — the usual grown-up stuff. Throughout, Amy clutched her mom's hand tightly and said nothing. She was almost invisible, sunken into the sofa cushions.

"Amy," Dawn said with a smile, "what's *your* favorite thing to do?"

Amy shrugged and leaned against her mom's shoulder.

"Would you like to see your room?" Mary Anne asked.

Amy shook her head.

"We have a bike for you," Dawn said enthusiastically.

Amy looked away and put her hand in her mouth.

Conversation with Amy went this way right through lunch. Amy ate three bites of the peanut-butter-and-jelly sandwich but wouldn't touch anything else.

Afterward, Dawn and Mary Anne took the Porters upstairs to Amy's room.

"It's beautiful!" Mrs. Porter gasped. "Oh, Amy, we're going to have to tear you away when we return!"

Well, the tearing away happened much earlier than that. It began the moment Mr. Porter said, "I guess we'd better hit the road."

Amy's response, more or less, was, "NOOOOOOOO!"

It was the loudest sound she'd made all day. Her mom knelt down beside her and said, "Now, Amy, it's only for a short time — "

"No, it's not!" Amy retorted. "It's *forever!* It's longer than *infinity!* I want to go with you!"

"Sweetheart, you'll have so much fun here," Mr. Porter replied patiently. "Dawn and Mary Anne will play with you and introduce you to girls and boys your age — "

"I hate Dawn and Mary Anne! All the kids here are old! I hate it here!"

Mrs. Porter picked up her daughter and hugged her. "Sweetie, you seem so angry."

Amy burst into tears. Her shoulders heaved up and down as she buried her head in her mom's shoulder.

Dawn could feel her own heart melting. Mary Anne cried silently, wiping her eyes with her fingers.

"It'll be worse for her the longer we stick around," Mr. Porter said softly to the rest of us. "Don't worry. In a little while she won't even remember who we are."

With a warm smile, he took Amy into a big embrace and kissed her. "Good-bye, honey. I love you."

"I love you, too," said Mrs. Porter, with tears streaming down her own cheeks.

"WAAAAHHHHH!" Amy replied, clinging to both of them.

Mr. Porter gently put her down. She collapsed on the floor, crying into the carpet.

Sharon, Dawn, and Mary Anne gathered around her. Richard took the car keys and quietly left with the Porters.

When the door shut, Amy shrieked and ran to the window. The glass pane fogged up as she called *"Mommy, come back!"* at the top of her lungs.

Mary Anne was a basket case. She grabbed a tissue box.

Dawn put a hand on Amy's back while Sharon tried to comfort her. Mary Anne wiped Amy's cheeks (and her own).

Oh, my lord, am I glad I wasn't there. Just thinking about it makes me cry.

Somehow they managed to pry Amy from the window. Sniffling and red-faced, she slumped onto the sofa. Dawn ran into the kitchen and brought back a cup of apple juice.

"I . . ." *Sip*. "Want . . ." *Sip*. "My . . ." *Sip*. "Dad and mom!"

"I know, Amy," Dawn said soothingly. "We understand."

Eventually they convinced Amy to venture out of the living room. By bedtime Amy had agreed to watch a video, eat some soup and bread for dinner, and listen to Dawn and Mary Anne read books before bedtime.

Halfway through *The Runaway Bunny*, Amy started weeping again.

"It's all right, Amy," Dawn said. "I feel homesick, too, sometimes."

"But you *are* home!" Amy replied.

"Well, yes and no." Dawn thought about explaining further, but she didn't. Thinking about California made her think about Mrs. Winslow. And that was just too upsetting.

Amy looked at her quizzically, but Dawn folded Amy into her arms and sang lullabies. Fifteen minutes later Amy was fast asleep. Dawn and Mary Anne lifted her into bed and tucked her in.

"Maybe she'll feel better in the morning," Mary Anne said with a sigh. "Anyway, she can't cry for three weeks."

Dawn nodded and turned away so Mary Anne wouldn't see the tears in her eyes.

CHAPTER 6

"Good luck, Stacey!" Mom called from downstairs. "I'll come see you!"

"Oh cur!" I called back. I meant "Okay," but I had a hanger in my mouth.

It was Monday morning at eight-thirty. Major SDT time. In an hour and a half I was to make my debut at Bellair's Kid Center. My new friends had come over on Sunday to celebrate my job (which did not thrill my mom), and Mia had given me a magazine clipping about summer jobs. One of the most important things, the article said, was first impressions. "Clothes make the employee," I had underlined. "On your first day of work, the wrong outfit can be as bad as the wrong attitude."

Great.

I needed something that looked smashing, could withstand crawling on the floor, and didn't show drool stains.

I scrutinized the mirror. The hanger in my

mouth held a pastel pink sundress. In my left hand was my striped nautical shirt and a pair of white shorts, in my right a blue cotton button-down shirt and khakis. Behind me on the bed was, well, just about everything else in my closet.

Anything white was out. A dress, too impractical. Shorts, too informal.

I put on the button-down shirt and khakis and ran downstairs before I could change my mind.

The strange thing was, I'd been nervous about finding a job. Now that I had one, I was even more nervous.

As I took out a grapefruit and began slicing, I gave myself a last-minute pep talk:

You've already been hired.

You enjoy taking care of kids.

This is only a summer job.

After a few bites and a glass of orange juice, my stomach felt like a mosh pit. I took a few deep breaths, brushed my hair, and prepared to leave.

RRRRRRIIING!

Arrgh. Just what I needed.

I picked up the receiver. "Hello!" I barked.

"Ooh, did we wake up on the wrong side of bed this morning?" asked Sheila's voice. "I just wanted to wish you good luck."

"Oh, sorry, Sheila. Thanks."

"What time are you off work?"

"About two o'clock."

"Great. Can't wait to hear how it went. Happy diaper changing."

"Thanks. 'Bye."

" 'Bye."

I hung up and hightailed out the front door.

Once again, I pedaled slowly to preserve my morning freshness. I arrived at Bellair's at nine-thirty and took the escalator to Mrs. Grossman's office.

She was busy trying to put together a plastic tricycle next to her desk. I knocked gently on the open door and called out, "Good morning."

"Hello, Stacey," she said, glancing up at the clock. "Aren't you dedicated to show up so early! Now you can see what a first-class klutz your boss is."

After watching her struggle with the trike for a moment, I volunteered, "Maybe the handlebar is backward."

Mrs. Grossman exhaled and sat back. "Be my guest. See what you can do."

Once, on a baby-sitting job, I had put together a similar tricycle. I lifted the handlebar out of its slot, turned it over, and put it back in.

Mrs. Grossman burst out laughing. "I knew I'd be happy I hired you."

Yea. I was off to a good start. (I didn't dare tell her I'd spent half an hour figuring out that same step the first time around.)

Mrs. Grossman gave me an official name tag and walked with me as I wheeled the trike to the Kid Center. A mother was waiting outside the locked door with a little boy.

"Ah, our first guest!" Mrs. Grossman said, unlocking the door. "What's your name?"

The boy said nothing. He ran inside and dived into one of the padded tubes.

"Joseph Harter," the mother said. "He's three, and I haven't left him with strangers before. I'm just not sure how he'll take this. He's shy."

"Weeeee!" squealed Joseph, sliding down a slide.

"He'll be in good hands," Mrs. Grossman assured her. "Now, Stacey, you need to sign each parent and child in, and fill out a name tag for Joe."

"Jofiss!" Joseph yelled as he headed for the trampoline.

Joseph's mom signed the sheet as I made a name tag. Mrs. Grossman watched over Joseph as he jumped and fell, laughing his head off.

" 'Bye, sugar!" Mrs. Harter scooped up her son and wrapped him in a big hug. "Don't worry. I'll be back soon."

"Bye-bye," Joseph said as his mom set him down. Then he ran to the wagon.

Mrs. Harter backed out of the room. She looked ready to cry.

"Sometimes the parents have a harder time than the kids," Mrs. Grossman whispered when Mrs. Harter had left.

I tried not to laugh. Joseph was having the time of his life, loading and unloading blocks on the wagon.

The next two children to be dropped off were Timothy and Brittany Taylor. Brittany was six, and she curled right up with a book. Timothy, on the other hand, was four, and he had his eyes on a set of wooden trains.

Unfortunately, Joseph was now lining them up on a track in an elaborate formation.

"Trains!" Timothy yelled, pouncing onto the track.

"*Noooo!*" protested Joseph. "Mine!"

Joseph grabbed the trains, but Timothy wouldn't let go. "You have to share!"

His sister sprang to her feet. "Timothy, you spoiled brat!"

Red alert. I ran to the boys. "Just a minute," I said, putting a hand on each of their shoulders. "I think these trains are sad. They're having a problem."

The boys glared at me. I gently took the trains and set them down.

"They don't know what to do without a driver and a stationmaster," I continued.

"I'm the driber," Joseph insisted.

"I'm stationmaster!" Timothy proclaimed.

"Excuse me, driver," I said. "Which trains report to the stationmaster for duty?"

Joseph stared at the trains for a moment. "These," he said, pushing four of them toward Timothy.

"Toooot-toooot!" Timothy yelled, coupling the trains on his side of the track.

"Well done," Mrs. Grossman remarked.

Brittany smiled at me. "Usually he eats baby-sitters for lunch."

"No!" Timothy burst out laughing. "She's a *person*, silly!"

Before long, two other assistants arrived. Their names were Sarah and Liz, and they were going into their senior year at Stoneybrook High School. Mrs. Grossman left, but promised to check on us from time to time.

I didn't have much chance to talk to my coworkers. The Kid Center filled right up. One little girl had an "accident" and her mother had to be paged. A five-year-old boy named Jerome sulked around, complaining that this place was "for babies." A dad brought in twin boys, along with markers and paper for them. The twins started using the paper. Then they decided to switch media. First they used each other's faces, then they progressed to the walls.

The other kids noticed before we did. Of course, they all wanted to join in.

Instant chaos. Time for damage control. Sarah and Liz took away the markers while I organized a mass cleanup.

You have never heard so many miserable kids. The twins wept. Timothy and Elizabeth argued. Jerome kept insisting he deserved to use the markers since he was "a big boy."

That was when my mom showed up.

"Uh-oh," she said. "Trouble in paradise."

"Mom!" I exclaimed. "Listen, can you please go to the kids' department and see if they have a face-painting kit? I'll pay you back."

"Sure."

Mom wasn't gone long. She managed to find exactly what I needed.

The face-painting was a huge hit. Jerome became a vampire, the twins were transformed into bees (don't ask me, it was their sugges-tion), and the others were an assortment of monsters and animals.

Sarah, Liz, and I took turns painting kids and scrubbing the walls. Most of the returning parents loved the face-painting, but Jerome's mom was annoyed because we hadn't cleared it with her first. I apologized and removed the paint with cold cream that was included in the kit. Still, she left in a huff.

It was two o'clock before I knew it. I didn't want to leave, even when Mrs. Grossman reminded me I could.

I finally said good-bye to everyone around two-twenty. It had been fun but exhausting.

And much harder than I had expected.

CHAPTER 7

"**H**ey, Stace-alita, how'd it go?"

I hadn't expected to see Jacqui on the up escalator as I was going down. But there she was, with Mia, Heather, and Sheila.

"Hi!" I called out. "Where are you going?"

"To meet you!" Heather replied. "Want to shop?"

"Wait for me up there!"

When I reached the bottom, I switched to the up escalator. My friends were waiting for me on the third floor.

"What a great job!" I exclaimed.

"Yeah?" Heather said. "Nobody barfed on you, or snotted up your shoulder? My little cousin does that all the time."

"Say it louder, Heather, so the whole store can hear," Mia remarked.

I laughed. "They found other ways to make a mess. But it was fun."

Sheila was not listening. She had walked

ahead, into the music section. "It's here!" she called over her shoulder.

"It," we all knew, was *U & Me 4 U4Me*, the latest CD from you-know-who.

We all ran to her and gaped at the display. It was Skyllo, life-size and lifelike.

Sigh.

Needless to say, we each bought a CD. And a U4Me T-shirt. And a special U4Me magazine on sale next to the display.

We raced back to my house (on the way, I made sure we bought snacks).

Eating chips and drinking juice, we listened to the CD over and over. By the third time we were singing along at the top of our lungs.

On Tuesday we had only one emergency at the Kid Center. A five-year-old boy disappeared from the room, but a saleswoman in Bedding found him bouncing on a king-size mattress.

Overall, though, the day was much smoother. Mrs. Grossman let us keep a face-painting kit in a cupboard, and she added a "No Markers" rule to a do's-and-don'ts list she was preparing for parents.

She told me she admired my "way with children," so I guess I was on the right track.

At one-fifty, I saw my friends waiting for me outside the Kid Center door, gabbing with each other and glancing at the clock. At two o'clock, Sheila started making "Hurry up" faces, but I was halfway through reading *Ferdinand* to a little boy, so I stayed until I was done. It was now ten after two.

"We thought you'd never stop," Sheila muttered as we walked away.

"Shei*laaa*," Heather said warningly.

"Ignore her," Mia said to me.

We took the escalator to the first floor. As we walked through Accessories, a gray-haired woman in a silk dress walked over to me, smiling. "You must be Maureen McGill's daughter!"

"Yes," I said.

Her name was Mrs. Ballmer, and she told me how much she enjoyed working with my mom. I introduced my friends to her, but they managed to slip away when Mrs. Ballmer started talking my ear off.

I finally broke loose and found them browsing together near the belts.

"Sorry about Mrs. Ballmer," I said as I approached.

"No problem," Jacqui replied. "Let's go eat."

The four of them headed toward the aisle.

"Did you find anything you liked?" I asked.

"Nahhh," Mia said over her shoulder.

I followed them. We left the store and went across the street toward Uncle Ed's, a fast-food Chinese restaurant.

Sheila and I arrived first. We were talking nonstop about U4Me (what else?) and paused only long enough to order our food. As we reached into our bags for our wallets, I noticed a gorgeous black-and-white silk scarf inside her bag.

"Oooh, where'd you get that?" I asked.

"It's for my mom," Sheila said, pulling out her wallet. She quickly closed up her bag and looked back into the restaurant. "You better pay for your order and then go save us some seats. It's crowding up."

"Okay." I paid the cashier, took a number, and turned around.

The place was half empty. I laughed. "Sheila, you are so paranoid."

"Yeah, Sheila," said Jacqui with a giggle.

Sheila was turning red. "Well, you never know," she mumbled, counting out her money near the cash register.

Each day my job became a little easier. On Thursday Mrs. Grossman told me I was "a dream to work with."

Boy, was I floating.

"What got into you?" Sheila asked as I

walked out of the Kid Center after work. (Yes, the Fabulous Foursome was waiting for me for the fourth day in a row.)

"My boss likes my work," I said.

"Congrats," Jacqui replied.

"I don't know how you can stand it," Sheila remarked. "I'd be smacking those brats."

"Yeah, *right*, Sheil," Mia said.

"Sheila's just cranky because she hasn't been shopping yet," Heather added.

I laughed. "You've been shopping every day this week!"

Jaqui shrugged. "There's nothing else to do."

I agreed. Sort of. Still, it *was* a little weird. I mean, I have had some serious shopathons, especially with Claudia. But four days in a row? In the same store?

Even I was impressed.

By now, I was getting to know a lot of the clerks. I couldn't walk through a section of Bellair's without someone calling out my name. Each time I stopped to chat, my friends would wander off. A couple of times I lost track of them, but I always found them together in one place. They never bought much. I figured they just enjoyed browsing together.

What a difference from the way the BSC used to shop together. Kristy would always organize us the moment we walked into the

74

store. We'd head off to different places, usually in pairs, then meet at some precise time in some precise place.

That day, as we were walking through Young Misses, I saw Mrs. Ballmer again, this time with a broad-shouldered man in a plain blue suit. They were scowling as they approached five high-school-age kids huddled together by a dress rack, giggling hysterically.

"Ugh, here comes Aunt Bea," Sheila muttered.

"What's she so grumpy about?" Mia asked.

The five kids suddenly looked up at Mrs. Ballmer and the man. Their faces fell.

"Uh-oh," Jacqui said under her breath.

"May I help you?" I heard the man ask the kids in a sharp voice.

The kids shook their heads. After a long, awkward pause, they slunk away.

As Mrs. Ballmer turned to leave, she spotted me and rolled her eyes, as if to say, "What a pain."

I smiled. Once, during a school work project at the mall, I discovered just how common shoplifting is. I knew that store managers often keep their eyes on suspicious-acting people and gangs of teens.

When I turned back around, my friends were gone.

"Sheil?" I called out. "Mia?"

I looked up the next aisle, but they weren't there. I walked around a large wall display of sportswear, and into Bellair's book department.

The four of them were in the thrillers section. I spotted Sheila looking at a paperback, then giving it to Heather. "Hey, guys!" I called out.

Sheila spun around. "Oh. Hi."

"What are you reading?" I asked. But when I was close enough to see Heather, she had nothing in her hand.

"I don't know, just some horror book," Heather replied. "Sheila likes them, not me."

"Oh," I said.

"Can we go now?" Mia asked.

Jacqui was already heading for the door. Sheila, Mia, and I followed her.

Behind us, I could hear the click of the buckle on Heather's shoulder bag.

My stomach began to sink. I imagined Heather taking away the book inside her bag. Stealing it.

Nahh, no way. I was just being oversensitive.

Then I thought about the time Logan Bruno started hanging out with a bunch of tough guys who liked to shoplift. They brought nice, innocent Logan with them on purpose, because shopowners wouldn't suspect them if he were around. In other words, they used him (the creeps).

Was that happening to me?

I looked back at Heather. She smiled. I didn't have the heart to say anything.

Now I was thinking about the scarf I'd seen in Sheila's bag. She hadn't taken it out to show me. Instead she'd sent me away to save a table. Why? Had she stolen it?

Sheila, Mia, Jacqui, and Heather were strolling out the front doors. Did they look a little tense? I couldn't tell.

Maybe I was being paranoid. These were friends of Andi. *She* would never shoplift.

I hardly said a word as we retrieved our bikes and said good-bye. All I wanted to do was talk to Robert. He'd known those girls longer than I had.

I felt funny talking over the phone about this stuff. So I didn't. But Robert and I had made a date for Friday night. I could wait a day.

I vowed to ask him in person.

CHAPTER 8

Thirsday

Today I sat for Miss droopy Drawrs. Honestly, Dawn and Maryann I dont know how you do it. I tride to be so simpa sympatet understanding. Was I to cereus or somthing?

If I ever have to sit for her agan, mabe I'll bring a woopee cushin . . . .

Thursday was Amy's fifth day in Stoney-brook. Dawn and Mary Anne had sitting jobs that afternoon, so Claudia was hired to take over.

When Claudia agreed to take the job, Dawn and Mary Anne gave her a detailed progress report:

Amy wasn't crying all the time anymore. Just most of the time.

She had smiled at least twice, first on Tuesday morning (during their visit to the Stones' farm) and then on Wednesday afternoon (during a video).

She sat through a movie at the cineplex but didn't want to talk about it afterward, hated everything on the menu at Cabbages and Kings, and refused to go to the museum.

She hardly even looked at Laurel and Patsy when they came over.

The news was not encouraging.

Claudia armed herself for the job. She brought along a satchel full of art supplies.

Thursday was clear, warm, and dry. Claudia felt optimistic as she rang the Schafer/Spiers' doorbell.

Grumpy and Dismal answered.

"Who died?" Claudia joked.

"Ha ha," Dawn replied.

"She's upstairs in her room," Mary Anne

said. "We can't convince her to come down."

Claudia shrugged. "Okay, so I won't expect hugs and kisses. I'll survive."

"Thanks, Claud," Mary Anne said with a sigh. "Just don't push her. That seems to make things worse."

They exchanged good-byes, and Dawn and Mary Anne left.

Humming to herself, Claudia went upstairs. "Hello?" she said, knocking on Amy's door.

No answer.

Knock-knock-knock.

"It's Claudia Kishi. Just wanted to say hi."

The door opened slowly. Amy looked at her blankly. "You're the baby-sitter?"

"Yup."

No response.

"And you're Amy, right? Nice to meet you. I brought some art stuff, if you're interested."

"Crayons are for babies."

"Crayons? No way, José. I brought colored pencils, really big paper, modeling clay, tempera paints — "

Amy stared at her for a second, then closed the door.

"Um, well, if you change your mind, I'll be in the den, okay?" Claudia said to the door.

Silence.

Claudia sighed, then wandered downstairs.

In the den, she put on a CD and opened a sketchpad.

She was humming along to the music, drawing a portrait of Amy from memory, when the door flew open.

Amy stood in the doorway with her arms crossed. "The music's too loud."

"Oh!" Claudia exclaimed. "You scared me."

"I can hear it all the way up there," Amy said.

"I'm sorry. I'll turn it down."

Claudia put her sketch on the sofa and walked to the CD player.

"Who's that?" Amy asked, looking at the sketch.

"Do you recognize the face?"

Amy shook her head. "Uh-uh."

"It's supposed to be you."

Amy's face fell. When she looked up at Claudia, her eyes were glazed with tears.

"What's wrong?" Claudia asked.

"You're making fun of me."

"No! Oh, Amy, I wouldn't do that in a million years. I just thought you were pretty and you'd make a good subject."

"But that doesn't look like me!"

Claudia smiled at her warmly. "Sit across from me. I promise I'll do a better job if I can see you."

Amy hesitated.

"I'll give you paper and a pencil," Claudia suggested. "You can draw me at the same time."

Amy's brow furrowed. She took a deep breath. "Oh, okay."

Claudia reached into her satchel and gave Amy a sketchpad and a charcoal pencil. Amy took it and sat in an armchair.

Claudia drew a little, looked up, drew a little more. Amy was pressing hard with her pencil, her tongue firmly in the corner of her mouth. It was difficult to see her eyes — and, as Claudia likes to say, "The eyes are the windows to the soul."

So Claud waited until Amy glanced up. When she finally did, she turned bright red. "I can't do this," she complained.

"Let's see," Claudia said.

"No!" Amy ripped off the sheet and crumpled it up.

"You seem angry about something, Amy."

"I am!"

"Well, why don't you try to draw how you feel? Just let your fingers express what you're thinking."

Amy glowered at her sketchpad. Then she started scribbling furiously, her tongue between her teeth.

82

As Amy worked, Claudia finished her sketch.

"Done," she said.

Amy looked up, and Claudia held up her sketch.

A smile flickered across Amy's face. "That's me?"

"Do you like it?"

"You're a good drawer," Amy said. "Can I keep it?"

"Sure. Now let's see yours."

Amy showed her an enormous scaly creature with bloodshot eyes. It was holding something that looked like a banana. Two stick figures were below the banana, floating with umbrellas like Mary Poppins.

Claud's heart went out to Amy. "Whoa. Scary. What's the creature holding?"

"A train. It's going to London, and the creature is picking it up and squashing it."

"And two people escaped?"

"Yeah. That's my mom and that's my dad. And that?" She pointed to the area beneath the monster. "That's Stoneybrook."

"Oh, Amy," Claudia said. "You want them back so badly, don't you?"

Amy lowered her head. Her hair fell in front of her eyes.

"It's just a vacation," Claudia went on.

"They're coming back. They love you."

"Then why did they leave me all alone?"

Claudia knelt next to the chair and put her arm around Amy's shoulder. "You're not alone."

Amy leaned toward her for a moment. Claudia thought she was going to cry.

Instead she stood up. "I'm not feeling too good," she said, walking toward the den door. "I'm going to my room."

As she slumped upstairs, clutching her portrait, Claudia couldn't think of a word to say.

CHAPTER 9

"So Gus gets permission from the owner of the house to cut away this big tree branch," Robert said. "Otherwise he can't reach under the eaves to paint."

"Uh-huh," I said.

It was Friday night. Robert and I were riding our bikes to Pizza Express. I was waiting for an opportunity to tell him about the incident at Bellair's.

"So we cut down the branch with a pole saw, and it crashes to the lawn," Robert went on. "And we see this shriveled-up little thing hanging from it."

"Yeah?"

" 'What's that?' I ask. Gus says, 'It's a nut or something. Like an acorn.' And I ask, 'An acorn on a maple tree?' "

"No such thing," I said.

"That's what I tell him. But he decides since he's a high school senior, he has to be right.

So he reaches down to pull it off — and turns absolutely white. You have never seen someone jump so far and scream so loud!"

"What was it?"

"A sleeping bat." Robert tossed back his head and howled with laughter.

I shuddered. "Disgusting!"

"That's only the beginning. Then the bat opens its wings and flies at him. Gus tries to scream and run away but it's too late. The bat grabs onto his neck and starts sucking his blood."

"Whaaaat?"

"Rank!" Robert pedaled ahead of me, laughing aloud.

I chased after him. We wound through the streets of Stoneybrook. By the time I caught up to him, he was grinning triumphantly in the parking lot behind Pizza Express.

I pretended not to see him. I locked my bike at the other end of the rack.

Robert sneaked up from behind and wrapped his arms around me. "What a bee-ooootiful neck you have, my sweet," he said in a terrible Dracula voice.

"Robert, you are so weird," I said. "I *didn't* believe you, you know."

"It was a true story," Robert insisted. "Up to the vampire part."

"Really?"

"Really." Robert took my hand and we started walking toward the restaurant. "It was the most exciting thing that's happened all month at work. This job is so boring."

"Why don't you apply to Bellair's?" I suggested.

"Nahh." Robert smiled at me. "I wouldn't be able to pay attention to the kids."

Suddenly Robert's stupid vampire story went flying out of my mind. I wish I could put that smile in an envelope and carry it around in my pocket. It's positively dangerous. His eyes start to dance, this little dimple creases his left cheek, and I turn into applesauce.

As we opened the door to Pizza Express, the noise slammed into us. The place was jumping. The jukebox blared a heavy metal song. About ten kids were waiting for tables by the cashier.

"Robert! Stacey!"

We turned to see Sheila and Marty Bukowski waving to us from a huge, round table on the other side of the restaurant. Mia was at the table, too, with a guy named Lew Greenberg, who's on the track team. At the table next to them were Heather, Jacqui, and two guys named Alex Zacharias and Peter

Hayes. Most of them were already scarfing down pizza. A few steaming slices were left at the center of each table.

As we approached, Lew grabbed two empty chairs while the others at the table shifted over.

"I *knew* you guys would be here!" Sheila exclaimed.

"Yo, Brew-doggy!" Marty called out, holding a hand high above his head.

"Bukeman!" Robert replied.

The two of them did this bizarre ritual handshake that involved a high-five at the top of a jump, a slap on the shoulder, and a few other things that I missed because I was looking away in embarrassment.

"They actually practice this stuff," Mia said, shaking her head.

"Another pizza, please!" Marty called to the waiter.

As soon as Robert and I sat, he began repeating his bat story. Everyone leaned forward to listen.

Me? Well, this wasn't exactly what I had expected. I'd been hoping Robert and I would be alone. But I couldn't be upset. We were with our best friends. Robert was having a great time.

Besides, we'd have a bike ride later.

We all talked nonstop and somehow managed to finish off the extra pizza in about two minutes.

At one point, Mia said, "Did you hear U4Me canceled all its midwest concerts?"

"Why?" I asked.

Mia shrugged. "I guess they were having too good a time on the West Coast or something."

"They once skipped a whole weekend at Madison Square Garden because Skyllo snuck away to go skiing," Sheila said.

"Their manager must have wanted to kill them," Alex remarked.

"They don't care what other people think about them," Heather said. "I think that's pretty cool."

"I think it's dumb," Peter Hayes volunteered.

"Why do boys always hate U4Me?" Jacqui asked.

"Jealousy," Sheila replied.

Marty, Alex, Lew, and Peter groaned.

"Who would be jealous of those dweebs?" Lew said.

"Uh-oh, here we go again," Heather muttered.

It was the Great U4Me Debate: girls on one side, guys on the other. Robert and I gave each other a Look.

"This is boring," he whispered.

I nodded. "Do you have any quarters?"

"I think so. Why?"

I pointed to the jukebox.

Robert nodded. We stood up and walked across the room.

"You pick," Robert said, stuffing coins in the jukebox.

I carefully pressed the numbers of two U4Me songs. As the first chords of "I Don't Wanna Say Good-bye" rang out, our table exploded with cheers and catcalls.

Robert and I laughed. I suddenly realized this would be a good time to talk to him about what was bothering me.

I put my arm around him. "Want to take a walk?"

"Sure."

Outside the air had turned cool. I leaned against Robert's shoulder as we strolled down the block.

Before I could bring up the subject, Robert said, "Stacey? You don't mind being with all my friends on our date, do you? Because we can leave if you want."

"Hey, they're my friends, too, you know."

Robert held me tighter. "Yeah. The girls really like you. I can tell. I don't blame them, either."

You see how sweet he is?

I tried to think of a way to tell him my suspicions. But I couldn't.

What was I going to say? *Robert, do you think our friends are shoplifters?*

I hate accusing people. Besides, Robert knew them. If he thought they were jerks, he would have dumped them long ago.

Maybe I just needed to get used to them. Sure, they were funkier than my old BSC friends. That didn't make them thieves.

As Robert and I walked back into Pizza Express, I decided to calm down and enjoy the rest of the night.

CHAPTER 10

That Monday, at two o'clock on the dot, Sheila appeared at the door of the Kid Center. It had been a pretty light day, so I was able to leave on time.

"Where's everybody?" I asked.

"In Designer Dresses," Sheila replied. "You know, dreaming."

I laughed. "Can I ask you a question?"

"Sure."

"Don't you guys ever get bored with Bellair's?"

"No way! I could live here," Sheila said, stepping onto the down escalator. "You are so lucky, Stace. I mean, you're here every single day, everybody knows you, you can see the new clothes before the general public does." She sighed. "I'll bet you even have a great employee discount."

"Ten percent. And next week the bathing

suit I want goes on sale, and I get the discount off *that* price."

The escalator slid us onto the second floor. In the distance, I could see the other girls browsing among the dresses.

"Stace?" Sheila said. "Do you think we could — Oh, never mind."

"What?"

"Well, some of the stuff here is so expensive, and I just thought, that discount would really make a difference, and, well, you know . . ."

"You want me to see if Mrs. Grossman needs another worker?" I asked.

"Mrs. Who? Oh, I didn't mean that! I was thinking, Heather and Mia and Jacqui and I have seen some stuff we like, and if you bought it with your discount, we could pay you back. Then we'd get a break on the price, too."

"I don't know if I'm supposed to do that, Sheila."

Sheila looked at me blankly. "What's the problem? Just one thing for each of us. Bellair's doesn't have to know who the clothes are for. They'll get their money, you'll get yours. Everybody will end up happy."

"Well, yeah. . . ."

"So it's okay, right? Unless you don't trust us to pay you back."

"No, I do. I mean, I guess it's all right."

"Stacey, you are such a good friend." As we approached the other girls, Sheila called out, "She said yes, guys!"

"All riiiiight!" Mia cried. She and Heather and Jacqui thanked me a million times.

As they pawed excitedly through the merchandise, I tried to look interested. The truth? I felt kind of weird.

I told myself it was a harmless favor. But what if my mother found out? She does work in the store offices, after all. Maybe she'd see a record of my purchases somewhere.

But that was a longshot. And I hated to force my friends to pay ten percent more than I would pay. So I went along with their suggestion.

"This is nice." Jacqui held up a beige silk robe with a Bellair's logo on the collar and a tasseled sash belt.

I imagined Jacqui wearing that, with her dyed hair and black nail polish. "Right," I said with a laugh.

"For my *mother*, Stacey," Jacqui replied.

She folded it over her arm. We walked toward Sheila, who was examining a low-cut, fringed, sequined dress. "This is like something out of an old movie."

"Yeah, but where would you wear it?" I asked.

Sheila shrugged. "I don't know. Some formal occasion."

Jacqui laughed. "The queen's ball."

"At least I'm not buying some polyester bathrobe."

"It's silk," Jacqui insisted.

They cracked up.

Hilarious. They couldn't have picked out normal clothes. They had to put a robe and a sequined dress on my bill.

We met Heather near the cashier's desk. She had picked out a pair of full-length calfskin gloves (she said it was a gift for her aunt). Mia showed up a moment later carrying a wide-brimmed black straw hat with an ostrich feather.

"Very chic," Sheila remarked.

"Ooh-la-la," Jacqui growled.

The four of them started giggling.

I laughed, too. Okay, so my friends were weird. That was no surprise. And *they* were going to shell out the money, so who was I to question their choices?

If someone from the front office ever asked, I could always say I was Christmas shopping early.

Actually, Halloween shopping might be more like it.

"Could you charge these to my employee

account, please?" I asked the cashier, giving her my employee card.

In a few minutes, the clothes were rung up and wrapped up.

My eyes popped when I looked at the receipt. Even with the discount, my friends owed me a small fortune.

My second week in the Kid Center was going smoothly. I wasn't worrying about my choice of clothes anymore (the older assistants usually wore jeans and T-shirts), and I had already made friends with a few repeat customers. On Wednesday, a little girl named Nadia threw a tantrum when I said I had to leave.

She finally quieted down when her mom arrived at quarter after two. By that time, my friends were sitting in the hallway, laughing like crazy.

Did you ever hear the expression "stage door Johnny"? That's a guy who waits for his actress girlfriend by the stage door after a Broadway show.

Well, I had my own stage door Johnnies. Or Kid Center Kates . . . or Daycare Daphnes? (Actually, they had missed Tuesday. And, to tell you the truth, I had missed them. It was lonely riding home all by myself.)

"What's so funny?" I asked.

They answered with a group giggle.

"We're taking you out to lunch, on us," Mia said.

"What's the occasion?" I asked.

"To celebrate Saturday's U4Me concert," Sheila replied.

"In Stamford," Heather added.

"Whaaaaaaat?" I practically shrieked. *"This* Saturday? You're joking!"

"No joke," Mia insisted. "You know them. They like surprises."

"Tickets go on sale at five o'clock," Jacqui said. "One of the outlets is at the strip mall, so we can camp out there after lunch."

Well, I was flabbergasted, to say the least.

"Go ask your mom," Sheila insisted.

We ran to Mom's office. She didn't seem thrilled about the idea, but she agreed to let me go. (Having four friends with me didn't hurt my cause, I'm sure.)

As we headed toward the escalator, we could not stop talking about the concert.

On the first floor, Sheila dug into her handbag. "Oh, here's what I owe you."

"Me, too," Heather said.

The four of them carefully counted out their money and gave it to me.

"Thanks, guys," I said. "I feel rich."

"Where do you want to eat?" Sheila asked.

"Uncle Ed's, I guess," I answered. "What

happened, did you win the lottery?"

They started giggling again. "Not exactly," Mia said.

"Lunch is your commission," Jacqui said. "To pay you back for Monday."

"You don't have to," I insisted. "You just paid me back. It's not like you made extra money."

"Oh, no?" Sheila said with a sly grin.

"Shei*laaaaa*," Mia warned.

Sheila rolled her eyes. "We're not going to keep it a secret, Mia."

"What?" I asked.

On the ground floor, Sheila grabbed me by the hand and pulled me toward the front door.

Outside the girls huddled around me. Sheila's eyes darted left and right. "We returned the clothes," she said under her breath.

"All of you?" I asked. I couldn't believe it. Jacqui and Mia had both changed their minds? Sheila's mom and Heather's aunt had hated their gifts on the spot?

"Don't worry," Mia added. "We didn't go together. No one suspected anything."

"Suspected what?" I asked. "I mean, people return clothes every day. I just don't understand why you didn't pick stuff you liked."

"Well, um, my aunt said — " Heather began.

"Heather, don't be a dork," Sheila snapped.

"Stacey, we brought them back without receipts."

"I had the receipt," I reminded her. "You could have asked me for it."

"Well, we said we'd lost it," Jacqui said. "They just went, like, 'Okay, no problem, we know you bought it here,' and gave our money back."

"Full price," Sheila added.

I stood there, frozen. I wished this were a video, so I could press rewind. Was I actually hearing this?

"You guys did this to make money?" I asked.

Sheila shrugged. "It's not much. Enough for a decent lunch, though."

"A decent — are you guys joking or something?" I said. "Because if you are, it's not funny!"

Mia rolled her eyes. "Stac*eeeey*, it's no big deal. No one will ever know the difference."

"But it's cheating," I replied. "It's like stealing ten percent of the price!"

"Come on, Stacey, don't be a baby," Sheila said. "They charge everyone full price. Are they stealing ten percent from *those* customers? No, right? Don't have a cow."

"I didn't know she was going to be like *this* about it," Mia muttered.

"Let's eat," Heather said. "I'm starved."

They started walking away, just like that.

Half of me wanted to apologize. The other half wanted to scream at them, then run home and never see them again.

Sure. Just what I needed. No friends to hang out with the rest of the summer. And who knows what they'd tell Robert? He'd already given up basketball, partly because of me. I didn't want to make him feel pressured to give up his friends, too.

Besides, Bellair's was a big company. Maybe they didn't care about stuff like this.

I followed them into Uncle Ed's. I was hungry, but I couldn't eat much. The food tasted all right. It just didn't go down easily.

CHAPTER 11

"Stacey!" my mom called from the bottom of the stairs. "It's for you!"

I had just pulled my U4Me T-shirt over my head. The back of it had caught on a barrette. As I tried to untangle it, I hopped around on the caved-in heel of a sneaker I'd tried to slip on without untying the laces.

It was Saturday night, a mere hour and fifteen minutes before the U4Me concert, and I was Toots, the Hopping Hunchback of Stoneybrook.

"*Stacey?*"

Finally my head burst into the atmosphere. "Okay!"

I hobbled into Mom's bedroom and picked up the phone. "Hello?"

"Aaaaaugh!" screamed Sheila's voice.

"Please, I need that ear," I replied.

"I am so excited. I can't eat! I can't talk! I

can't breathe! I am going to have a heart attack."

"Give me your ticket. I can sell it at the door."

"How can you joke around at a time like this?" I'd never heard Sheila like this. She was hyperventilating. "I just wanted to be sure you didn't forget to pick me up!"

"Oh, Sheila. We do have over an hour. Relax. We should be by in about fifteen minutes."

"I'll be waiting on the porch. 'Bye."

" 'Bye."

I stumbled back to my room to finish dressing.

In case you're wondering: Yes, I was still friends with Sheila and the others. Yes, we had managed to buy five seats together. And yes, we had had to wait in line for a humongous amount of time.

At least *I* had.

After we'd left Uncle Ed's, we biked to the outdoor mall. It's the old-fashioned kind, built in a long U-shape. Usually it's not too crowded at that time on a weekday. But we could hear the ticket line about three blocks away.

"Single file, please," a voice called through a megaphone.

"Oh, my lord," I murmured as the line came into view.

The place was a mob scene. The ticket line began at Sound Ideas, a music store at one end. It snaked around the entire U, all the people tucked neatly behind a row of police sawhorses.

"This is going to take forever," Mia remarked.

We picked up speed. A moment later we hopped off our bikes and attached ourselves to the back of the line. About twenty more people joined behind us.

For awhile it was kind of fun. One girl in line had a boom box, and she played the new U4Me CD. We must have met twenty new people.

An hour later, we were halfway to the ticket booth. Sheila began complaining about her tight sneakers. Mia's arms were tiring from holding up her bike. Heather said she was feeling claustrophobic.

"My mom's going to kill me if I miss dinner," Jacqui said.

With a frustrated sigh, Sheila announced, "I'm going to take a ride." As she climbed on her bike, she handed me her money. "If I'm not back in time, can you buy my ticket?"

"Sure," I agreed.

"Me, too," Jacqui said, mounting *her* bike.

Soon Heather and Mia did the same thing. I was glad I'd met some other people in line.

Otherwise I would have spent the next half hour completely alone. I ended up buying all five tickets myself.

Boy, was I furious.

That feeling lasted until I went to sleep that night. That's when it dawned on me: I, Stacey McGill, was going to see U4Me. In person. Breathing the same air as Skyllo. Hearing his voice, live.

I was a wreck. I could not sleep.

Now, on Saturday night, I wasn't thinking about the ticket line at all. I was trying to force my sneaker over my heel.

"Stacey? Are you off the phone? We don't want to hit traffic."

"Okay!" I jammed my feet into my sneakers, fixed my hair, checked my shirt for stains, grabbed a cotton sweater, and left.

I took the stairs three at a time. Mom watched me in awe.

"I wish you were this fast with the chores," she muttered as I whizzed past her and out the front door.

Our transportation was all set. Mom had agreed to drive us to the concert, and Mia's older brother would pick us up.

First stop was Sheila's. She was sitting on the curb, clutching a manila envelope.

She pulled the door open almost before the

car stopped. "Hi!" she said, throwing her arms around me.

"What's that?" I asked.

"Photos. You know, for signing."

Mom laughed. "I thought you were sitting all the way in the back."

"*Afterward*. I'll stand outside the stage door all night if I have to," Sheila said.

"Or at least until your ride comes," Mom said as she pulled away.

Next we picked up Jacqui, who was wearing a floppy black hat, skull earrings, and a rhinestone nose ring. She was carrying a handmade sign that said:

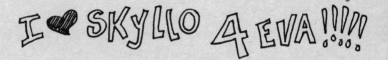

Mom laughed at that until I called her "Paula." That quieted her down.

After picking up Heather and Mia, we headed for Stamford. I had brought a few U4Me cassettes, which Mom let us play during the trip.

Traffic slowed to a crawl at the exit ramp, but it didn't matter. We were surrounded by friends — hundreds of kids our age were hanging out of car windows, rocking to U4Me, waving banners, singing songs.

Mom dropped us off near the entrance to the concert hall. As we piled out of the car, she called out, "Call me if you need anything!"

"Okay," I replied.

"Watch out for pickpockets!"

"Yes, Mom!"

"Oh, Stacey? Do you have your injection kit?"

Now people were turning around and staring. I was so embarrassed.

"Yes, Mom! 'Bye!"

" 'Bye! Have fun!"

We were already running through the crowd. I could barely feel the ground beneath me.

CHAPTER 12

*T*WAANNNNNNNGGGGG!

We could hear the warmup group practicing inside. In front of us were about half a million kids, waiting impatiently to be let through the ticket gate.

What did we do? I can barely remember. I know Sheila, Jacqui, and I were gabbing, but chances are we were making no sense. Mia and Heather were wearing headphones, dancing to tapes on their portable players.

A drum riff floated out from the arena, and everyone cheered.

As we inched closer, I could see why the line was taking so long. Inside the turnstiles, guards were questioning certain kids, mostly heavy metal types who looked high-school-age or older. Some of the kids were being pulled over to the side. I saw one guard holding a liquor bottle and directing a guy out a side exit.

"Tough security," Sheila remarked.

On a concrete pillar near the turnstile was a huge sign. It said NO on top, followed by a list underneath that included LIQUOR, SMOKING, PETS, SKATES, and MOTOR VEHICLES.

Whew. Good thing Mom didn't try to drive inside.

Finally we passed through the turnstiles. While the guard ripped our tickets in half, he glared at a loud group of teens behind us.

We tore across the ground floor and took the escalator up . . .

And up . . .

And up . . .

Our seats weren't on the top level, but they were close.

But who cared? The minute I walked into the seating area, my heart started pounding.

The warmup band, Third Rail, was just starting its first song. They were pretty good, but the show was dull.

We found our seats and settled in. It was much warmer in there than it was outside, so I peeled off my sweater.

"Not bad!" Mia shouted.

"They stink!" Jacqui shouted.

"I mean the seats!" Mia replied.

"I should have brought binoculars!" Heather remarked.

"We won't need them!" Sheila said. With a grin, she reached into one of her white flop socks and pulled out a small bottle. "This is guaranteed to improve vision."

At first I didn't understand. Maybe I'm just dense. Or naive. You wouldn't expect it of me, being from New York City.

But for a teeny moment, I thought Sheila had smuggled in a bottle of cough syrup.

Laughing, Mia reached inside her shirt and took out a bottle of her own.

Jacqui had one in her hat.

Heather's was tucked in the lining of her jacket, which was conveniently ripped on the side.

"Cheers," Sheila said.

She sat back in her seat and took a swig. One by one, the others did, too.

My jaw hit the floor. "You have alcohol in there?" I asked.

"No," Sheila said, "prune juice."

The others thought that was so funny, they started howling.

"Want some?" Heather offered. "It's just wine."

"No!" I shot back. "How can — "

"She *can't*," Sheila snapped at Heather. "Where did you park your brain? Alcohol has sugar in it, remember? Stacey's a *diabetic*."

"Sugar?" Heather said. "No kidding?"

"Duh," Sheila replied, looking at me as if she expected me to find that funny.

Well, I did not find it funny at all. Far from it. And it had nothing to do with my diabetes.

I had never seen them drink before. Not at Pizza Express, not at their homes, nowhere. None of them had even talked about it. And now they were lifting the bottles, in full view of everyone, as if they did it every day of their lives.

How did they get the liquor? When did they decide to bring it? Why hadn't they told me? How long had they been drinking? Were they just doing it tonight, to look cool?

I wanted to ask a million questions. Sheila must have been reading my mind, because she asked, "You don't mind, do you? I mean, I kind of feel bad you're left out."

"No, it's not that, Sheila — "

Sheila let out a deep sigh. "You're not going to freak out again, are you, like you did outside Bellair's?"

"Well, no," I said. "But this is different."

"Oh, Stacey." Mia sounded totally disgusted. "We're minding our own business. We're not hurting anybody."

"You don't have to do it if you don't want to," Heather added. "We respect you, so you respect us. Simple. So just chill. We're here to have a good time."

A good time. Right. Just sit there and enjoy the music while my four friends get drunk. No problem.

I really wanted to let them have it. But I didn't. I kept my mouth shut. It wasn't as if they were the only ones ignoring the rules. I could see other kids sneaking bottles and cigarettes around.

Still, that didn't make it right.

I could see guards lurking in the shadows, too. That made me nervous. Breaking the stadium rules was bad enough. But drinking underage?

This was just plain stupid.

Not to mention illegal.

What could I do?

I could storm away. But then I would miss the concert. My money would be wasted. I'd have to call my mom and wait for her in the dreary parking lot. Then I'd have to make up some explanation — rat on my friends or dream up some lame excuse. Either way I'd be sure never to see my friends again. And they would bad mouth me in front of everybody, including Robert.

I sat back and tried to ignore them. Hey, if the guards saw them, they would be in trouble. Not me. I had warned them. I told them how I felt.

SCREEEEEEEEEE . . .

Third Rail was starting to annoy me. They played endless guitar riffs. Their music was monotonous. Their lead singer had the personality of a turnip.

"Boo!" Sheila shouted. "Off the stage!"

"U4Me! U4Me! U4Me! U4Me!" Mia started chanting.

Soon our entire section had joined us. Heather, Jacqui, Sheila, and Mia were screaming.

Finally I joined them. Sheila smiled at me. Winking slyly, she asked, "Sure you don't want just a little bit?"

"No, thanks."

"Even a sip? That'll mess you up?"

"Well, I did bring my injection kit."

"Ew."

I knew that would shut her up.

Before long, Third Rail was off the stage. Sheila was now passing around a cigarette and talking to some kids in back of us.

When U4Me finally hit the stage, the place went berserk. I thought I could feel our section of the stadium move. Skyllo didn't emerge until halfway through the first song. He descended in a cloud of smoke from the rafters. Don't ask me how he got up there. I wasn't thinking straight.

I felt as if I'd died and gone to heaven.

We were on our feet, singing as loudly as we

could. U4Me sounded even better in person than they did on a CD. And even though Skyllo looked about the size of a fruit fly from my seat, he was making my spine tingle.

The drinking? It wasn't bothering me anymore. Nor anyone else. All around us kids were bumming bottles from time to time. No one was rowdy. Everyone was cool. Open. It was as if we'd all known each other for years.

As good as I felt, my friends seemed looser, happier. I imagined a video camera panning over us. It would see Sheila and the others in their funky clothes, humming along, moving to the music. From time to time they'd take a sip.

In the corner of the scene would be me, sitting with my sweater folded in my lap.

In my little video, I looked like a total nerd.

By the fifth song, Mia and Heather broke into a fit of giggles. Sheila kept trying to ask what was so funny, but that just made them giggle harder. So Sheila started giggling. Jacqui tried to shush them, but she ended up joining in, too.

After awhile, they were so loud, it was hard to tune them out. "Yo, keep it down!" someone called from behind us.

Sheila stood up and turned around. "What do you think this is, a library?"

"Mind your own business!" Mia shouted.

"Easy, guys," I said urgently.

A balled-up candy wrapper hurtled down toward us.

"Hey, keep your trash to yourself!" Sheila scooped it up and threw it back, but her toss was way off course, and the wrapper bopped some innocent guy on the head.

He snarled at Sheila and turned away.

Sheila pointed her bottle at him. "Who are you looking at?" she called.

I grabbed her arm and yanked her down.

Then someone grabbed mine.

"Excuse me, miss," said a deep voice. "Could you step into the aisle?"

I whirled around. A security guard was pulling me toward him. He looked past me toward my friends.

Sheila's mouth was hanging open. She tried to hide her bottle behind her.

Mia was in mid-sip. She hadn't noticed a thing yet. Heather and Jacqui had turned their backs and were busily scrambling to hide their bottles.

"Could you young ladies step out here, please?" he asked.

Crash! Sheila's bottle hit the floor. Even in the dark, I could see her face turning red.

Sheepishly, my friends walked into the aisle, empty-handed.

I was sweating like a pig. I fought back tears

as the guard pulled up our seats and found two bottles. Then he started rummaging in our stuff.

When he turned around, he was holding my sweater. Slowly he unfolded it and pulled out a flask.

My heart stopped.

"Whose sweater is this?" he asked.

"It's hers," Jacqui said, pointing at me.

The guard glared at me. "Is it?"

"Well, yes — I mean, no!" I stammered. "The sweater is, but not the bottle!"

I looked at Sheila. She didn't say a word. Mia, Jacqui, and Heather were all staring glumly at the floor.

"Take your possessions and follow me, please," the man said.

I was shaking as he led us away from our seats. Behind us, U4Me was playing "I Don't Wanna Say Good-bye." We walked through the brightly lit concession area to a small office.

The security guard sat us around an old metal table. A bored-looking woman in a blue uniform introduced herself as Ms. Breen, head of security. She asked us our names and ages.

"I wasn't drinking!" I blurted out. "I was just watching the band. Tell her, you guys!"

Total silence.

"Your name, young lady?" Ms. Breen asked.

"Stacey. Stacey McGill. But look, officer!" I opened my shoulder bag and pulled out my injection kit. "I'm a diabetic. I couldn't drink, even if I wanted to."

The woman didn't seem interested. She passed a sheet of paper to each of us. "Do you understand that what you did was illegal?" she asked.

Sheila, Mia, Heather, and Jacqui nodded.

"You're not going to call the police, are you?" Sheila asked.

"No, not this time. But I will call your parents. Just fill out these forms, please, and I'll need a parent's phone number from each of you. I will explain exactly what happened and arrange a pickup."

"Can't my brother pick us up?" Mia asked.

The woman just shook her head.

I felt dizzy.

We were in deep trouble.

CHAPTER 13

I don't know how long we waited. I couldn't look at a clock because my eyes were glued to the floor. None of us spoke.

Mr. and Mrs. Pappas were the first to arrive. You should have seen the looks on their faces. If I had been Mia, I would have preferred staying in the security office to going home.

"We're letting them go with a warning this time," said Ms. Breen. "If they're caught again, the police will be notified."

"You're being too generous," Mr. Pappas snapped.

Mia didn't even look up as she left.

A moment later Mrs. MacGregor walked in. Ms. Breen gave her the same talk. Sheila started sobbing uncontrollably.

Both she and her mom were brushing back tears as they left.

When my mother arrived, I nearly lost control. Her face looked drained of color, as if she expected to find me dead. When she saw me, relief passed across her eyes for a split second, right before turning to fury.

My knees shook as I stood up. Ms. Breen introduced herself, and before she could go into her speech, I said, "Mom, they found a bottle in my sweater. But I didn't put it there. You know I wasn't drinking. Tell her."

Mom shot a murderous look at Heather and Jacqui. Then she turned to Ms. Breen. "I can assure you that my daughter does not drink. If she'd had even a small amount, she would be having a diabetic reaction right now."

"I understand," Ms. Breen replied. "She's not the first girl to suffer for her friends' mistakes."

"Thank you," Mom said. She walked to the door and held it open, glaring at me.

I swallowed hard.

When I was seven, Mom bought me a pair of expensive white patent leather shoes, which I insisted on wearing home, promising to be careful. Of course, I promptly stepped in a grimy New York City mud puddle, right in front of her. I will never, ever forget the look on her face.

This was like that look, only worse. Much worse. I half expected her to spank me on the way out.

Before I could say a word, she stormed

across the floor toward the exit. I had to run to keep up with her.

"Hurry up," she called over her shoulder. "I'm parked illegally."

Our car was on a grassless hill at the side of the parking lot. A ticket had been placed on the windshield. Mom groaned, snatched it off, and climbed into the front seat.

"Sorry, Mom," I said.

"What do you expect?" she retorted as she started the car. "The lot is supposed to be closed. I drove in through the exit."

She edged off the hill. The car scraped bottom as it jounced onto the lot. "Do you think I enjoy driving to Stamford and back twice in one night?"

"No," I murmured.

"Besides," she went on, "that's not all you have to be sorry about."

"But I was telling the truth, Mom. I didn't do anything wrong."

The car lurched to the right as Mom steered out of the lot and onto the road. "Anastasia McGill, I brought you up in New York City. From the time you were a little girl, you could size up a suspicious person half a block away. But you still can't figure out when your own friends are using you."

"Using me? For what? They were just being jerks, Mom. They probably knew I'd be mad about the alcohol, so they kept it secret till the last minute."

"So why didn't they tell you in advance and give you the choice to go with someone else? It's not only that they're inconsiderate. They *needed* you to go with them. Think about it, Stacey. Look at you. You dress nicely, you look clean cut and friendly. If I were going to a concert to drink, you'd be the perfect person to take with me past security. Those ticket takers wouldn't give you a second look."

Whoa. That struck home. I thought about all those afternoons in Bellair's. Those afternoons when I'd chat with store personnel and my "friends" would circulate through the store. And leave with scarves and paperbacks and who knew what else.

Boy, did I feel stupid.

Mom sighed as she drove up the entrance ramp to the expressway. "These are some friends. They freeload off you at home, they plant themselves outside your place of work every day, they abandon you on the world's longest ticket line, and then, as a reward, they use you to help them break the law. What next, Stacey?"

I wanted so badly to tell her about their scam at Bellair's, but all I said was, "I won't let them do it again, Mom."

Mom was silent for awhile. It was starting

to rain, and the drops sounded like the drumming of impatient fingers. "Look, Stacey," she finally said. "I can't control your personal life. You have to make your own decisions. But when you blow it, I have to do my job. You are grounded for the next three days."

"Okay," I squeaked.

"And as your mother, I would like to put in a simple *request*: that you consider never wasting another nanosecond of your life with those girls." She glanced at me quickly, then looked back to the road. "You understand that this is merely a request."

I understood, all right. Loud and clear.

I was lucky. My grounding was not quite total. Mom let me go to work Monday and Tuesday.

Of course, my Daycare Daphnes had disappeared. Each day I could walk out the door into an empty hallway.

It felt great.

I did not miss my "friends" one bit. Mom was absolutely right. The more I thought about it, the angrier I became. And you know what the worst part of it was? Their silence in the security office. Even after they were caught, they still wouldn't back me up.

I talked to Claudia once on the phone. She listened and was sympathetic, but I knew she thought I was crazy for hanging around with those girls in the first place.

I couldn't wait for Wednesday. Then I'd finally be able to see Robert. We'd talked on the phone, too, of course. At first I'd been afraid to mention anything. I thought he'd try to defend his friends. But he listened quietly as I described every detail.

"Wow, I can't believe this," was his response. "I mean, I knew Sheila was kind of a sneak. And Lew said that Jacqui had lied to him a lot. But Lew's no saint either. I guess I just never really bothered to know them."

"I'm sorry, Robert," I said.

"Why?"

"Well, I know they're your friends and all — "

"Hey, I'm on your side, Stace. Don't worry. I won't forget how rotten they were to you. And you know what I'll say the next time one of them asks *me* for a favor."

"Thanks, Robert. Love you."

"Yeah. Me, too."

I should have felt all warm and happy inside after our talk, but I didn't.

I liked what Robert had said. But he *hadn't* said he'd stop being friends with his old crowd. And that bothered me.

What would happen the next time we wandered into Pizza Express and saw them at a table? I sure wouldn't sit with them. But I couldn't force Robert away from Lew and Alex and Wayne, his best friends.

What was I going to tell Andi when she came back? I had no idea. I tried not to think of her.

I wished I could flop down on Claudia's floor at a BSC meeting and collect everybody's advice. But those friends were history, too.

I'd never felt more miserable in my life.

CHAPTER 14

Wednesday

Today was the scariest day of my life. I nearly had a heart attack. I thought taking care of Amy couldn't become any harder than it was. But boy, was I wrong . . . .

Mary Anne Spier does not usually write things like that. When Claudia read the passage to me over the phone, I thought she was kidding at first.

But Mary Anne was dead serious.

Wednesday was the day my grounding ended. I celebrated by visiting Robert on my way to work.

At Mary Anne's and Dawn's house, it was Day Seventeen of the Amy Porter Ordeal. Poor Amy was still miserable. (Poor Amy? Poor Mary Anne and Dawn!) Every day, Mary Anne would think of a new place to visit, or Dawn would invite some other kid over to play. Sometimes Amy showed a flicker of interest. But it never lasted long.

Patsy and Laurel Kuhn refused to return to the house after their first rotten visit. Mal Pike's sisters, Claire and Margo, called Amy "Gloomy." Gloomy Porter.

Most of the time Amy watched TV, lingered over her food, and read books. Sometimes, when she'd hear a car outside, she'd scurry to the front window and stare out of it for a long time.

The Porters sent her a few postcards. Reading them, Amy would grin from ear to ear. But her spirits would always sink afterward, and she'd go back to moping around the house.

On Wednesday, as she ate a bowl of cereal, she asked, "Dawn? Do you think they like London?"

Dawn nodded. "Sure. Remember the plays they told you about? And the gardens and shops and museums?"

"Is it more fun than Chicago?"

"I don't know," Dawn replied. "I've never been to either place."

"Me, neither," Mary Anne said.

"Do a lot of people live in London?" Amy asked.

"Millions," Dawn answered.

Amy finished her cereal silently.

Once again, Dawn and Mary Anne went through their daily Amy ritual. A little Monopoly Jr., a game of checkers. A couple of house chores, a video. Candy Land.

Zzzzzzz.

Amy seemed even more withdrawn that day, if such a thing were possible. At one point she darted upstairs to her room without any explanation and closed the door behind her.

A few moments later she reappeared and asked, "Can we play outside?"

Play outside? Mary Anne and Dawn were elated. Amy hardly ever suggested anything herself.

"What did you have in mind?" Dawn asked as they hustled out the back door.

"Hide-and-seek," Amy said. "You guys are 'it'!"

"Both of us?" Mary Anne asked.

"Yes. And count to fifty."

"Okay!"

They turned toward the house and counted in unison. "One . . . two . . . three . . ."

They heard her running around the yard. But by the time they reached fifty, the noises had stopped, and Amy was nowhere in sight.

Now, the Schafer/Spiers' is about the best place in the world to play hide-and-seek. The yard is gigantic, the barn has lots of crannies, and some of the trees are huge and gnarly.

Mary Anne checked the barn. (She even peeked into the secret passageway, but no six-year-old in the world would think of entering that alone.)

No Amy.

"Hmmm, I think I'm getting warmer," Dawn called out as she ran through the yard, peeking around corners.

Mary Anne dashed into the house and looked in all the rooms.

Dawn checked the basement.

They met in front of the house. "She's good," Dawn said.

"Amy?" Mary Anne called out. "We give up!"

They walked around to the back of the house.

"*Amy?*" Dawn repeated. "You can come out now!"

Silence.

"*Aaaamyyyyy!*"

Across town, I had just arrived at work. It was Liz's eighteenth birthday, and Mrs. Grossman had brought a small cake.

I couldn't eat any, but two lucky little boys had shown up, and their parents gave us permission to feed them some. (Which was, of course, bad news for the carpet.)

As we were cleaning up, the Kid Center filled up. I carefully kept track of the name tags and sign-ins.

One woman walked in with a boy and girl behind her. She signed *Sandy Frederickson* under the "Parent" column and *Randall* under "Child."

"And your daughter?" I asked.

"Excuse me?" she replied.

"Your daughter's name?" I glanced at the little girl.

She turned. "Oh. She's not mine. See you in about an hour!"

I counted the children in the room. Seven.

I counted the signed-in children.

Six.

Now, something like this had happened before. A five-year-old boy had wandered in while his mom was shopping nearby. So at any moment, I expected a frantic parent to run in looking for the girl.

She was wandering around the room now, examining the toys, heading in Liz's direction. "Excuse me!" I said, approaching her.

She turned. "Where's the train station?"

"Train station?" I repeated. "Well, we do have some trains. What's your name?"

"I thought this was where the train station was. But it's a store."

"Uh, yes, you're right. But you — "

"So where is the train station? I don't see it."

"You have to give me your name first."

She rolled her eyes. "Amy."

"Is your mommy or your daddy shopping here today, Amy?"

"Nope. They're in London."

Bing.

The lightbulb finally went on.

"Whoa, wait a minute," I said. "Is your last name Porter?"

She cocked her head. "How did you know?"

"Are your cousins here?"

"No. They're 'it.' "

I had no idea what she was talking about.

As Amy wandered off, I pulled Liz aside and asked her to watch Amy while I made a call.

On the Kid Center's wall phone, I tapped out Mary Anne's number.

"Hello?"

It was Mary Anne. She sounded frantic. Even so, my throat parched up at the sound of her voice. We hadn't spoken a word in so long.

"Hello, who is this? Amy? Is this you?" That was Dawn, on the other extension.

What were they doing at home? *How had Amy come here?*

"It's Stacey. Um, Amy is here at the Bellair's Kid Center. She's fine."

"How did she get there?" Dawn demanded.

"I have no idea. She asked about a train to London or something."

"Oh, my lord," Mary Anne whispered.

"Keep her there, Stacey," Dawn said. "We're on our way."

Click.

Butterflies came to life in my stomach. They crashed around as if they had metal-tipped wings.

Did I *have* to be there when Mary Anne and Dawn showed up? Maybe I could visit Mom. Liz and Sarah could cover.

If not, I could disguise myself with the face-painting kit.

No. I had to be professional. My first priority was to be with the kids.

Besides, I was dying to find out what had happened.

About twenty minutes later, Mary Anne and Dawn burst into the Kid Center, red-cheeked and breathless. They didn't even look at me.

"Amy!" Dawn cried out. She ran to her cousin and lifted her in a tight embrace.

"No! No! No! No!" Amy cried out, flailing her arms and legs. "I'm not going back!"

Without even thinking, I reached for a tissue box. I managed to hand it to Mary Anne before the first cascade spilled off her cheek.

Dawn held tightly to her cousin. Amy stopped fighting and dissolved into tears.

"It's all right," Dawn whispered, rocking her for a moment.

Now Liz and Sarah and I were starting to cry. Around us, most of the other kids played as if nothing were happening.

Gently Dawn set her cousin down. "Where did you go?" she asked carefully.

"Here," Amy said with a sniffle.

"Did someone drive you here?" Mary Anne asked.

"No. I walked and ran."

Dawn looked stunned. "You sneaked out while we were counting?"

Amy's eyes darted away. "I'm not going to live with you forever."

"I know," Mary Anne said. "Your mom and dad are coming back on Saturday to take you home. So why on earth did you run away?"

"You're tricking me. You said they were coming back but they didn't. So I'm going to them. But I have to find the train first."

Dawn let out a deep breath. "Amy, London is across a huge ocean. You can't take a train there. And you must absolutely never, *ever* run away like that. Do your parents let you walk on the streets alone in Chicago, or cross them by yourself?"

Amy stared at the floor. "No."

"Well, we have the same rules here! *Don't let me ever —* "

Tears fell from Amy's eyes, making dark splatters on the carpet. Her lip was quivering.

Dawn's voice hitched. She stopped her speech and hugged Amy again.

Mary Anne turned to me for the first time. "Thanks, Stacey."

"Yeah," Dawn said, rising to her feet. "You really saved us."

I could barely force a "You're welcome" around the lump in my throat.

CHAPTER 15

I made a decision that Friday.

It started as a germ of an idea when I saw Dawn and Mary Anne at the Kid Center.

It grew over the next couple of days, whenever I thought about Sheila, Mia, Heather, and Jacqui.

I was thinking about friends a lot. I sure didn't have many now. I tried to imagine what the perfect friend would be like. I made a rough list:

Smart.
Funny.
Cool.
A fabulous dresser.
Someone who likes to shop.
A good listener.
Someone who makes me feel good.
Someone I enjoy making happy.

That's all. Simple.

Sheila and her gang sure didn't pass this test. By a long shot.

And except for Claudia, neither did the BSC members. Each of them was lacking maybe one or two ingredients. Mary Anne, for instance, isn't exactly cool. Dawn's not the world's greatest listener. Kristy certainly didn't always make me feel good.

So why was I missing them so much? Why had it felt so good when I saw Mary Anne and Dawn? I kept asking myself those questions, until I had an answer.

Together, the members of the Baby-sitters Club had all those qualities. In spades. The balance tipped from time to time (sometimes a *lot*), and it had really swung to the uncool side before I left. But that didn't mean it couldn't tip back again.

Anyway, when I finally made my decision, I called Claudia.

"Claudia," I said, "you're not going to believe this. I want to join again."

"Uh, excuse me?" Claudia said. "Could you repeat that? I think this is a bad connection. I actually thought I heard you say you wanted to join the Baby-sitters Club."

"I do. I mean it. Do you think the others would take me back?"

Claudia let out a long, low whistle. "Whoa. Let me talk to them at the meeting, okay? I'll call you right after."

By six o'clock, I was a mess, pacing my room, biting my fingernails. When the phone rang, I nearly hit the ceiling.

"Hello?" I said.

"What are you doing Monday at five-thirty?" Claudia asked.

"They said yes?"

"I didn't say that."

"What happened?"

"Well, I told them you wanted to join. No one threw a tantrum or fainted or barfed, which I thought was a good sign. Dawn and Mary Anne told everyone what happened at Bellair's. They were all impressed that you were still involved with kids. I guess they thought you'd turned into an ogre or something. So they asked me to invite you to the meeting. You still want to come?"

"Are you kidding? Invitation accepted!"

I was feeling pretty terrific that weekend, but I still needed to clear up one thing.

It took me all day Saturday to work up

enough courage to approach my mother about it.

Before dinner, I told her about the scam Sheila and the other girls had pulled at Bellair's — the clothes bought on my account, the returns without receipts. Also, I said that I suspected that they may have also shoplifted from Bellair's, though I couldn't really prove it.

Mom buried her face in her hands. Then she sighed and sat back on the sofa.

"Profiteering, too," she remarked. "Thanks for telling me, Stacey. That must have been hard to do. I'm proud of you."

"What should I do?" I asked.

"Report it, first thing Monday. Otherwise, an audit may pick up the loss, and some clerk may take the blame. My gut feeling is the company will absorb it. They're not going to chase after those girls."

"Okay, Mom."

I have to admit I was a little disappointed. I was kind of looking forward to the idea of Sheila sweating it out in court.

I did report the incident on Monday. The store manager thanked me. She insisted no one would be punished, but she would think about instituting a store policy of requiring receipts on all returns. "Up till now Bellair's has been lenient," she said, "but people like your friends spoil it for the rest."

Ex-friends, I wanted to say.

That evening, at 5:28, I entered Claudia's room for a Baby-sitters Club meeting.

I could have heard more lively "hellos" in a funeral home. I sat cross-legged on the floor and tried not to look too scared.

"Ahem. Order!" Kristy said at precisely five-thirty. "Any old business?"

"Dues day!" Shannon called out.

I started to reach for the envelope but stopped myself. It felt strange to see someone else doing my old job.

After the money was collected, Kristy said, "Any new business?"

"Well, Amy's back in Chicago," Dawn said. "When her parents showed up, she could not stop jumping. She hugged her dad so hard his glasses broke."

"The first thing her mom said," Mary Anne reported, "was 'I *knew* she would have a good time here!' "

Everyone groaned.

"Well, I move we bring up the topic of Stacey," Claudia said.

No one said a word.

Finally I spoke up. "I guess I should make it official. I would like to join again. I'm sorry for the mean things I said. I want to work things out."

No one reacted, except Mary Anne. Her eyes started misting over.

"I move to consider Stacey's re-memberification," Claudia said.

Kristy rolled her eyes. "Application for membership."

"That, too," Claudia said.

"I second," Mary Anne spoke up.

"Third," chimed in Jessi.

"Are there any objections?" Kristy asked.

Dawn nodded. "What about Robert, Stacey?"

"Well, I'm still going out with him," I replied. "But I think I can work my personal life around sitting. I'm determined to."

"And you don't think we're babies anymore?" Kristy asked. "That's what you called us, you know."

"Look," Claudia said. "She says she wants to join. She's sorry she hurt people's feelings. She made some mistakes. She promises to do better. And she's one of the best sitters around. What's the argument?"

"Well," Kristy replied, "I guess we could have, like, a probation period or something. I mean, see how things go. But no special treatment, Stacey. Show up on time. No last-minute switches."

I nodded. I would have preferred some high-fives or a group hug. But this was a start. I had to take what I could get.

Rrriiiing!

"Hello, new and improved Baby-sitters Club," Claudia said. "Yes, hi, Mrs. Hobart. When? Saturday? Let me check."

Mary Anne flipped through the record book. "Well, Kristy's at the Kuhns' and Jessi and Mal are sitting for the Pike kids. But you're free, Claud and Dawn." Mary Anne looked up. "And how about you, Stacey? Are you working at Bellair's that day?"

"No, I'm not working there anymore. I didn't want it to conflict with my club responsibilities."

As Mary Anne scribbled something in the book, I couldn't help smiling. It felt great to be back in the club.

About the Author

ANN M. MARTIN did *a lot* of baby-sitting when she was growing up in Princeton, New Jersey. She is a former editor of books for children, and was graduated from Smith College.

Ms. Martin lives in New York City with her cats, Mouse and Rosie. She likes ice cream and *I Love Lucy*; and she hates to cook.

Ann Martin's Apple Paperbacks include *Yours Turly, Shirley*; *Ten Kids, No Pets*; *With You and Without You*; *Bummer Summer*; and all the other books in the Baby-sitters Club series.

Look for #88

FAREWELL, DAWN

"Dawn!" Sunny screamed, recognizing my voice.

"I was missing you and wondering how your mom is feeling."

"I'm cool, but Mom is still in the hospital."

"How's she doing?"

"Better," Sunny replied. "The doctor said she hopes Mom can come home next week."

"That's great."

"Yeah, it is," Sunny agreed, but her voice was quiet and unsure. "I mean, she's not definitely coming. They have to run more tests and all."

More than anything else I wished I could be at Sunny's house right that very second to put my arm around her shoulder. It's hard to be there for a good friend when you're not *there* in person.

"That stinks," I sympathized. "Tell her I hope she feels better soon."

"So, how are you?" Sunny asked cheerfully, changing the serious mood.

"Everything's fine here," I said, "but do you ever wish you could be two places at once?"

"Sure. Wherever I am I always wish there was another me who could be at the beach."

That made me laugh. "Well, I wish one of me could be here and another one could be in California."

"Are you coming back?" Sunny asked, sounding hopeful.

"No," I told her. "But I'd sure like to come, at least for awhile."

Sunny and I talked some more, mostly about the kids I used to sit for when I was part of the We ♥ Kids Club. The more we talked, the more I longed to be there.

Finally, I said good-bye and sat down at the kitchen table with my salad. As I ate, a frightening realization came to me. At first, I didn't want to think about it and just kept pushing it out of my head.

But the insistent thought kept coming back. There was no getting away from it.

As much as I loved living in Stoneybrook. I wanted to move back to California.

Permanently.

Read all the books
about **Stacey**
in the Baby-sitters Club series
by Ann M. Martin

THE BABY-SITTERS CLUB®

by Ann M. Martin

More titles... ▶

The Baby-sitters Club titles continued...

Available wherever you buy books...or use this order form.

Scholastic Inc., P.O. Box 7502, 2931 E. McCarty Street, Jefferson City, MO 65102

Please send me the books I have checked above. I am enclosing $_____
(please add $2.00 to cover shipping and handling). Send check or money order - no
cash or C.O.D.s please.

Name _____ Birthdate_____

Address _____

City_____ State/Zip _____
Please allow four to six weeks for delivery. Offer good in the U.S. only. Sorry, mail orders are not
available to residents of Canada. Prices subject to change.

BSC993

Coming to theaters this summer!

THE BABY-SITTERS CLUB® MOVIE

Big things are happening in Stoneybrook and the cameras are rolling....
It's a major motion picture based on your favorite books and starring your favorite baby-sitters!

And don't miss this!
Look for four all-new, never-before-published BSC books based on the big screen adventures of The Baby-sitters Club Movie, and jam-packed with plenty of photos from the film.

Tell your friends about **The Baby-sitters Club Movie.**
Opens nationwide this summer.

BSCM1194